Adrenaline surged t

Her legs were free, and she twisted, trying to escape, but the other man still had a firm grip on her, one hand on her mouth and the other across her chest.

"Grab her feet!" one attacker snapped. "Don't mess this up."

"He said this was an easy job," the other man growled.

Ellie sucked in breaths between the fingers of the man's gloves, trying not to hyperventilate. They were going to take her somewhere. As soon as she left this greenhouse, barefooted, her chances of getting away would dwindle.

Please.

"Put. Her. Down!"

Her eyes darted to the door in time to see Michael charging through it.

"Put her down and get off my property," said Michael, standing over her. "I'm only saying this once." His authoritative tone left no question that he would take action. He had been so careful with her, but now she saw another side, equally protective. This man was ready for anything.

Rebecca Hopewell is the kiss-only pen name for an award-winning romance author. In addition to writing, she loves to read, wander in the forest and talk with friends and family. A perfect day is when she manages to do all four of these things! Rebecca lives just outside San Francisco.

Books by Rebecca Hopewell

Love Inspired Suspense

Danger on the Peaks

Love Inspired Mountain Rescue

High-Stakes Blizzard

Visit the Author Profile page at LoveInspired.com.

Danger on the Peaks

REBECCA HOPEWELL

LOVE INSPIRED SUSPENSE
INSPIRATIONAL ROMANCE

LOVE INSPIRED® SUSPENSE
INSPIRATIONAL ROMANCE

ISBN-13: 978-1-335-59821-9

Danger on the Peaks

Recycling programs
for this product may
not exist in your area.

Copyright © 2024 by Rebecca Hopewell

For questions and comments about the quality of this book, please contact us at CustomerService@Harlequin.com.

® is a trademark of Harlequin Enterprises ULC.

Love Inspired
22 Adelaide St. West, 41st Floor
Toronto, Ontario M5H 4E3, Canada
www.LoveInspired.com

Printed in Lithuania

MIX
Paper | Supporting
responsible forestry
FSC® C021394

Peace I leave with you, my peace I give unto you: not as the world giveth, give I unto you. Let not your heart be troubled, neither let it be afraid.
—*John* 14:27

To my father, who has supported me in my career
and in countless other ways. I love you!

ONE

She opened her eyes. It was dark, but above her, she could make out a low, rocky ceiling, uneven and damp in the dim light. Cold. She was cold. The chill from the uneven ground below her seeped through her clothes. Something poked at her back. She looked to one side then the other, taking in the dark rocks that surrounded her. She in…a cave? Why was she lying in a cave?

She lifted her head to sit up but froze as the dull throb at the back of her skull began to pound. Propping herself on one elbow, she reached behind her head with her other hand and touched the spot that the pain radiated from. She winced as her fingers touched something wet and sticky. She squinted at the dark red on her fingertips in the dimness. Blood.

Slowly, she pushed herself to sitting, trying to ignore the throbbing at the back of her head. A wave of nausea passed through her, starting in her stomach and traveling up to her throat. Not a good sign. A few deep breaths and some of the nausea subsided. Good. She needed to get up, to keep going, to protect herself.

Protect. The word ran through her mind, setting off a cascade of uneasiness, an unsettled feeling that something was wrong. Really wrong. She needed to find somewhere where she was safe. Because she wasn't safe here. The idea turned inside her and she tuned in to that feeling deep down that her life had been fundamentally shaken. She drew in a quick breath as a surge of energy took over, a drive to run, to escape, but when she tried to focus her mind, to grab hold of details, some basis for this fear, there was nothing there—just a hazy, nebulous dread that burned through her.

Standing seemed like a dangerous proposition at this point. Better to stay low to the ground until the nausea ebbed. She faced the dim opening of the cave and began to scoot herself forward. She stretched out her legs then lifted her body forward with her hands. Once. Twice. If she moved slowly, her head didn't throb as much, so she continued toward the entrance. As she drew closer, she could make out the general view: a sky thick with heavy clouds, more rock, and a light layer of new snow covering sets of footprints. The latter was strange—how many times had she wandered in and out?—but nothing she saw was particularly helpful in jogging her memory. She stopped a few feet from the snow, brushed off her hands and touched the back of her head again at the tender spot. The blood was dark enough to make her suspect that she'd been lying in the cave for a while.

She stared at her hand, at the blood, searching for some inkling of how she'd gotten to this point. How could she not know? She turned her hands over to inspect them. Her nails were a pale beige and the polish looked fresh and unchipped. As she took in the details of her fingers, something caught her eye. There was a faint tan line across the fourth finger of her left hand, lighter than the rest of her skin, as if a wedding ring belonged there. Except there was no ring. A truth appeared in her head, fully formed, certain and unbearably heavy. Her husband was dead. She was a widow.

The idea was a punch to her gut, and she doubled over as

pain and fear grew into a tidal wave that crashed over her. Stars appeared as her vision faded into blackness, threatening to sweep her under forever. And then, just as suddenly as the emotions came on, they faded into a haze in her brain, leaving only that unsettled feeling that something was wrong. Deeply wrong. Everything else was gone.

She blinked as new understanding set in. It wasn't just where she was or how she'd gotten there that was a mystery. She didn't know *who* she was either. A new wave of panic rose inside her, enough to make her gasp. What had happened to her?

"It will all come back in a minute," she whispered aloud. "It *has* to."

The sound of her own voice was grounding, familiar. She took a steadying breath. There had to be something else familiar around her, something that would trigger her memories. She looked down, taking in more details about herself. Gray wool slacks, fancy lace-up black boots that weren't holding up well in the weather, and a darker gray wool coat… Why was she wearing nice clothing in a cave? She patted herself down and shoved her hands in her jacket pockets, searching for personal items. From one pocket she pulled out two snack-size bags of almonds, and from the other, a folded wad of tissues and a car key. The Cadillac logo on the fob was familiar. It was hers, that much she was certain about, but no memories of the specific car—or where she'd left it—came to mind. She stared at the contents of her pockets, bewildered. These items were so practical, and yet she hadn't brought along the basics like a phone or a driver's license. Did she have a handbag?

She swung around to search the cave floor and her headache pounded back to life. She squeezed her eyes closed until it receded. Opened them again. This time she took it slower, peering into the shadowy corners. The cave was empty. No handbag in sight.

Her stomach growled. She was hungry and thirsty, in that order. Maybe, after a little food and water, her memories would come back. She tore open one of the bags of almonds and gobbled them up. The turn of her stomach told her that it had been a while since her last meal. She moved to open the second bag then reconsidered. How far was she from more food? It was probably best to save it. Instead, she scooped up a handful of snow that looked clean and put it in her mouth, letting it melt. It chilled her throat enough to make her shiver. Which was the greater danger, dehydration or the cold? She grabbed one more handful, swallowed the icy liquid, and resisted another.

Instead, she tried to focus again. Her name? Her family? Where she lived? All of that was gone, and the more questions she asked herself, the more she realized she didn't know. Her identity, her memories, her life—all of it was gone.

She swallowed as a new wave of uneasiness ran through her, edged with dread, telling her there was danger outside the cave, too. She tried to search her mind for where this feeling was coming from, but it was as if a fog hovered over her memories, dark, dense and impenetrable. She could stay in the cave until some clue about herself came back, but how long could she do that with no food?

Her breaths were coming in shallow pants, and each beat of her heart signaled a warning, loud and relentless. *Run.* Stars flickered on the edges of her vision, dark and fuzzy, as her chest tightened…

"Please, Lord, help me." She whispered the words aloud. Just speaking them was cool relief from the torment of her thoughts. She had God, and the thought comforted her. Her voice itself and the words of prayer were hers, something to hold on to.

She took a long, steadying breath and blew it out. Again. Her heartbeat slowed and the panic ebbed in her chest. She could breathe again. That one thought turned her fear into determination.

She was going to figure this out. Every time she panicked, she was going to focus every ounce of her energy on the thought that God was there for her, even at a time like this. Especially at a time like this.

She looked outside again, this time attempting to study the landscape clinically. Though the boulders obscured her view, she was pretty sure there was a downhill slope. She leaned forward, sticking her head out of the cave, and the tops of tall pine trees came into view. Was she in the mountains? If she ventured out a little farther, maybe she could get a better view, just enough to see if there was some sign of civilization around. She'd turn around before she panicked because the cave, however cold and hard, was at least dry. And whoever she was scared of hadn't found her. Yet.

She glanced down at her boots again. They were too fancy to wear for a run through a snowy forest. Which meant that running through the forest was the last thing she had thought she would be doing today. At least she wasn't wearing heels. It was the first positive thought she'd had since she'd awoken, and she held on to it.

Determination mixed with a burst of energy from the food. She took one more handful of snow, letting the icy water cut a trail down her throat, then pushed up to standing slowly. Her head only gave a slight protest. She took a step into the snow, fighting the fear that pumped through her.

"Ignore it," she whispered and focused on what was in front of her.

Despite the warnings going off in her head, she continued, making tracks in the fresh snow. She stopped just before rounding the boulder, debating what she should be looking for. Somewhere with food, where she could take shelter from the cold. But if she found a place, how would she know it was safe? And therein lay the crux of the problem. Without her memory, she'd need help, but how did she know who was safe?

"One problem at a time," she muttered to herself. "Worry about that when you actually find shelter."

She peeked around the boulder. Heavy fog masked the landscape, a misty blur of white and gray. Nothing in sight was jogging her memory. The clouds rolled over the mountain, dark, thick puffs that engulfed the trees. She was lost in the clouds, both literally and metaphorically. The corners of her mouth tugged up at the thought. At least she hadn't lost her sense of humor, too.

Downhill seemed like her best bet, so she took a step forward. Another. Just as she rounded the thick boulder, she caught a flash of movement out of the corner of her eye. But as she whipped around to look, a large black glove clamped over her mouth. She couldn't move. She could barely breathe. She screamed into the cold leather, then gasped for air and screamed again, but only a muffled cry came out. The person—his deep grunt told her it was a man—tightened his hold.

Who was this man waiting outside a cave for her?

He pulled her against his chest with his other arm. Her heart skittered as she fought against his grasp, trying to get loose. She used her elbows to jab backward but, between her wool coat and the puff of the man's down jacket, it was impossible to land anything that mattered. Panic was taking over again. She tore at the arm clamped around her waist, but he was bigger and stronger than she was. It wouldn't budge. She kicked behind her and found the hard bone of his shin with her soggy boot. He grunted out a curse.

She froze as his voice resonated inside her. She knew that voice. *I know my attacker.* The panic rose like a tidal wave then crashed down on top of her. Stars edged her vision and her body sagged…

God is with me. That truth, strong and clear, echoed in her mind.

The man shifted and she was startled back to consciousness. Escape. The only thing that was important right now.

She dragged her legs under her, stomped on his foot and pushed backward. It worked. He stumbled back until their movement came to a jolting stop as they hit something. The boulder. The man's arm loosened from her waist, flailing at the edges of her vision. He was losing his balance, falling, and he was taking her with him. He stumbled and tipped, and let out another curse in that same, sickeningly familiar voice. She froze as the panic spiked inside her. Stars came back, closing in again. This time, she fought against it, fought against whatever memory was surfacing as they both hit the ground with a thud. Her head pounded and she gulped in another breath of air. She wriggled and scrambled away and screamed.

"Help! *Help me!*"

She climbed to her feet, her sopping-wet boots slipping in the packed snow, and behind her she heard the rustling of outerwear. He was right behind her. Her knees buckled. She hit the snow.

No. She would not crumble under this fear.

She stood and ran downhill, into the fog. Everything inside her wanted to turn around, to see the man who had captured her, but she knew she couldn't. If she turned back, she'd never escape.

The wind swept up the mountain in an icy gust and snow stung her face. She squinted out into the storm as she plowed through the snow, looking for something besides trees and rocks. Her head throbbed and her legs felt like they were disconnected from her body. How long could she run like this? But as she rounded a clump of low trees, she caught a glimpse of something else on the mountainside below. Was that…a shack? A cabin? It disappeared behind the clouds as quickly as it appeared. Had she imagined it? She wasn't sure, but still she ran toward that spot, willing the clouds to part again.

Finally, they did. It *was* a cabin, or at least some sort of small shelter with windows, made of weathered gray boards, the same color as the rocks around her. She braced herself for the fear that had crashed into her, that sickening familiarity, but it didn't come. So she ran for the shelter with everything she had.

"Help! *Help me!*"

Michael Tang jolted in his saddle as the cry carried down the mountain through the wind.

He had been making his way up the snowy trail, but the moment he'd heard that voice, that cry for help, he'd given Dusty a kick and the horse had picked up her pace. Snow covered the forest, hiding the rocks and shrubs, but both Michael and Dusty could find the trail with their eyes closed. He'd chosen the mare today for that reason, along with the fact that she had both endurance and sense. She was used to the snow, used to making her way through hidden trails. It wasn't the first time Michael had ridden this trail in the snow, on the lookout for stray cattle or stray backcountry skiers who'd somehow lost their way. But this cry didn't sound like a wandering tourist's. It was urgent, frightened. And it had cut him straight to his heart.

Even now, two years after Sunny's death, Michael still woke up at night thinking of how much his wife had suffered in the end. The house, the stables, the trails—everything was a reminder of the life Sunny had wanted and lost.

But this wasn't the time to think about the past. Right now, someone needed help, urgently, and the snow was coming down harder. It was easy to get lost in the mountains on a day like this, and the temperature was dropping. His father had heard some sort of argument earlier, which was why Michael had come out to investigate. That cry was still running through Michael's head in a loop he couldn't turn off. All of this added up to something he wanted no part of. Still, he wasn't the kind of man who could ignore it, so he shut down all the emotions welling up inside him and focused on the storm.

Dusty rounded another switchback, turning into the wind, and big wet flakes slapped Michael in the face, finding their way under his Stetson. Two days ago, the sun had been out, melting the winter layers, but now the snow was back. *Avalanche weather.* The heavy snow was piling onto the soft, unstable layers of late winter thaw and, when it got too heavy, it would all come sliding down the mountain. Michael's grandfather had chosen the location of their ranch wisely, farther down the slope, at the far side of the valley and out of avalanche territory. Yet the same couldn't be said for the newer subdivisions a mile or two above their property. He made a point of staying away from the higher trails during this time of the year, but today was looking like the exception.

The line camp appeared in front of them and Dusty's

pace slowed out of habit. The camp was nothing much, just a little cabin next to a stream and an outdoor corral with troughs for the horses to drink while they rested. Next summer, when the ranch was fully converted to a tourist ranch, some new hire would take the visitors here. Michael would be long gone by then. Emotions swirled in him. He tried not to think too hard about leaving when he knew this was best for his parents, the only way he could be a good son for them. Instead, he focused on the cabin emerging through the snow in front of him. It made a perfect location for someone to take shelter in a storm, which made it the most obvious place to start looking.

Michael tugged the reins as they approached the camp, bringing Dusty to a halt. He searched the ground around the cabin door for prints, but as far as he could see, the snow looked untouched.

"Let's go around," he told Dusty, tugging her reins to the right and giving her a little kick. The horse responded, starting toward the forest, but as they approached the corner, Michael caught a flash of movement in the forest. He brought Dusty to a stop and squinted through the snow, straining to get a better look. Bright red hair was the first thing he saw, lots of it. A woman appeared through the veil of white, and she was running toward him. She was wearing a gray coat, the fancy kind that wouldn't do much on a day like this, and her pants looked about the same. Her shoes were buried in the snow, but he was sure they were equally inappropriate for running through the winter forest. And she was running at full speed.

Michael knew the moment the woman spotted him because she came to a stop not far away, just ten yards or so. She stared at him, her gaze filled with fear. The woman was more striking than pretty, he couldn't help noting, and everything about her suggested money. Lots of it. Her dark eye makeup was smudged at the tops of her pink cheeks, giving her a haunted look. She glanced behind her, as if someone was on her tail, then looked back at Michael again.

"I need to get away from here. On your horse."

Her voice was low and urgent, and he had to strain to make out her words over the wind. It took a moment for him to process her request.

"You want my horse?" He would have laughed if she hadn't looked so desperate.

"I need to get away from here," she repeated, hurrying toward him. "Far away."

"Do you know how to ride?"

The woman hesitated. "Yes… Yes I do." She said it almost as if the answer had taken her by surprise.

Was she lying out of desperation or was there some other reason she'd hesitated? The whole situation was odd and made him uneasy. And yet…it touched on something inside that he thought had died along with Sunny. The urge to protect. Michael pushed that thought out of his mind. *Focus on the person you can help, not the one you can't.*

"I'll take you down with me. Get on back," he said, taking his foot out of the right stirrup.

After one more look over her shoulder, she approached the horse, letting Dusty sniff her, then came around to the side. Up close, he could see constellations of brown freckles that dotted her pink cheeks and forehead. Her eyes were dark gray, and her red hair was covered in a halo of white snow. He couldn't ignore the lines of deep concern across her forehead. She looked…desperate.

Michael reached out his hand and she took it. She slid her foot into the right stirrup and lifted herself up onto the horse with an ease that confirmed her words: she'd ridden before.

She put her hands on his waist. They were shaking, maybe from the cold or maybe from fear. That same instinct from before echoed inside him. *Protect her.*

"Let's go," she said urgently.

Michael had no idea what he was getting into with her, but he trusted that he was doing the right thing; that feeling that came from deep inside his heart, or what was left of it. He used to call the feeling a trust in God, but after Sunny had died, after the devastation of that loss, he wasn't sure he trusted God with anything anymore. Still, right now, he knew he was doing what he was supposed to do.

"Hold on," he said over his shoulder. He gave Dusty a swift kick and they were off.

Downhill was more dangerous than up in these conditions. The path had been trampled flat by decades' worth of rides, at least for the most part. But the snow hid stray rocks, fallen branches and other hazards. Dusty moved faster now, and the sudden turns of the switchback upped the horse's chances of slipping. Still, the mare knew her way, and when Michael leaned into the turn, the woman was right there with him. Yes, she definitely knew how to ride.

The storm was getting worse, and as they came to the road that ran through his family's property, the forest on the other side was a faded green blur, the driveway to the ranch a narrow patch of white. Gusts of wind shot down the open two-lane road, slapping his cheeks. He ducked his head and urged Dusty across. The woman's grip tightened around his waist and he felt her tense behind him. When they reached the driveway on the other side of the road, she tugged on his coat urgently.

"I hear a car," she hissed over the wind.

The faint hum of an engine droned, but it sounded like it was farther down the road. "Okay?"

"We have to hurry. Get around the bend."

He turned to glance at the woman. She was looking over his shoulder, like she was trying to assess their location, and there was fear in her eyes, fear his heart told him to listen to.

He gave a low whistle and nudged Dusty with his heel. The horse gave a snort then picked up speed. Michael navigated them down the driveway, toward where it curved around the stream that ran through the ranch. When they passed the first stand of tall pines, Michael drew back the reins. Dusty slowed to a stop and Michael turned them to face the road. They waited in silence, peering up the driveway. The woman shivered behind him.

"You need to get warm," he said over his shoulder.

She shook her head, snow fluttering from her fiery hair. "I need to know if someone is coming for me."

It was a fair point, but her shivering was getting worse.

Michael heard the engine slow before he caught sight of the vehicle hidden in a frosty cloud of snow. It was a large, white truck; the kind contractors favored, with black beams above the flatbed where someone might hang a ladder. The truck lurched to a stop directly in front of the driveway. Michael shifted, searching for something more identifiable on the vehicle, but the details were lost in the blowing snow. The engine quit and the passenger door opened. Someone in a dark jacket and dark hat stepped out, and the person appeared to be studying the ground.

An uneasiness crept up Michael's spine. The person from the truck was looking for something—or someone—and by the way this woman sat, frozen against him, he suspected it was her. Did the snow and the forest camouflage them? Maybe, though the woman's bright hair wasn't doing them any favors. If he could see the truck, the man could surely see them if he looked down the driveway...

The woman shuddered behind him, and Dusty shifted. He patted the horse's neck.

"Be still," he whispered to the horse.

A mumble of conversation made its way through the wind.

"We need to go," said Michael. "Hold on."

Before the woman could respond, he signaled Dusty to turn toward the ranch. They took off down the snowy driveway, making their way along the river until they came to a patch of boulders far out of sight from the road. Michael brought the horse to a stop again and looked back at the woman. She twisted in the saddle, studying the path behind them.

"Hey," he said, getting her attention.

She turned to him, her eyes wide.

"Who's chasing you?"

TWO

The man's voice was gruff but gentle, and she could see from his expression that she had his full attention. He was wearing a cowboy hat, a thick brown coat, and boots that looked much warmer than hers. His eyes were as dark as midnight, his cheekbones were high, and his clean-shaven jaw was set in hardened determination. The man's demeanor was reserved, but there was compassion in his eyes that broke through his stoicism. Quiet and yet devastating.

She didn't know this man, and she had no idea where they were. Still, somehow she felt safer as she sat there behind him. Somehow, riding with him made the panicked thumping of her heart slow. Could she trust him when she couldn't be sure of anything? Right now, all she had was her trust and her faith.

But his question set her heart racing again and she had no idea how to answer it. Why had she been so afraid of the sound of the truck? She searched her mind for something, but it was as if thick, ominous clouds had descended over her memories. How in the world could she explain this fear that pumped through her, the headache that slammed back each time she tried to follow that fear toward something more specific? She had nothing to go on except instinct, and instincts were bombarding her as the vision of the truck and the man who'd stepped out of it played through her mind. Amorphous fears were a paralyzing cacophony clambering for her attention. The one that sounded loudest was the danger that called from every movement in the snowy landscape.

"Who are you running from?" he asked, and this time his voice had an urgency to it.

Whoever was chasing her could catch up. She needed to work with this man, give him something that would convince him to keep moving.

"I don't know." Her voice came out steadier than she felt.

The man raised his eyebrows and she couldn't tell whether or not he believed her. If he didn't, if he gave up on her, then she was on her own again. And she was trying so hard not to lean on him—not yet. What if her instincts were wrong? What if this was dangerous, too?

You know self-defense, she reminded herself. *Trust yourself. Trust God.*

Self-defense? Where had that thought come from? A snippet of a memory came to her—the room covered with dark mats, the scent of sweat, the strain of her muscles as she took down her opponent—and then it was gone. The nausea from the cave returned with a vengeance, that sickening feeling that something terrible lingered just beyond the hazy cloud over her mind. She swallowed, trying to stave off the panic. The little bag of almonds—that had helped last time.

"I'm sorry, but I'm quite hungry," she said, shoving her hand in her pocket. She took out the second bag of almonds and tried to rip it open with her teeth, but her hand shook too much to get the right grip.

"I'll get that for you," said the man, taking it out of her hand.

He ripped the package open and laid it back in her palm. She poured half of it into her mouth, chewed hungrily, then ate the other half.

He was still watching her when she looked up again.

"I should have offered you some," she said sheepishly.

The man waved off her comment. "Let's get you indoors."

She let out a shaky breath and nodded. It meant they were heading forward, away from where that man had attacked her, away from where that white truck had stopped.

"I'm Michael," he added.

She opened her mouth to make something up, but a name popped into her head. Her own name—she was sure of it. "Ellie. My name is Ellie."

Her voice was filled with too much surprise for such mundane information, but he didn't comment on it.

"Those are about the worst winter shoes I've ever seen, Ellie. Your feet have to be frozen."

They both looked down Dusty's flank at the sorry state of Ellie's boots sagging around her ankles. He was right. She wasn't going to make it far in those. Her teeth chattered. All the running and panic had helped to drive away thoughts of the cold, but it was settling in again, deep inside.

"I can't be around other people," she blurted out. She knew she was acting strange, but anyone could be dangerous.

He gave her another look, like he was assessing what she was saying. Like he was taking her concern seriously. The tight grip that fear had on her insides eased a little. "There's a greenhouse in the back of the house that no one uses this time of year. It has a heater, and you can wait there while I get you some dry boots and a better coat. I'll get some food from Isabel, our chef, but other than that, no one needs to know you're there."

Warm, dry boots—a tantalizing thought that once again called attention to the fact she could barely move her toes. Michael turned back to her, watching her with those serious eyes. *Do I trust this man?* Her heart was telling her yes.

"Okay," she said before she could change her mind. "Thank you."

The horse made its way along the snow-covered driveway next to the stream, lined with snowbanks from previous storms. Ellie peered through the trees, starting at each unexpected movement as icy gusts of wind found their way under the layers of her coat. It felt like they were being watched. Was someone truly lurking out of sight, or was she just jumpy? The blanks in her memory so easily turned into fear.

The snow was falling steadily in fat wet flakes that melted on her coat. She patted the springy curls that were alarmingly visible in the periphery of her vision—her hair must be sticking out at both sides.

Ellie searched for a way to probe him for information without…well, sounding like she was probing. And confused.

"Has the ranch been in your family for a long time?"

"Depends on how you define long," he said, adjusting his Stetson. "We've owned it since Chinese Americans were allowed to own land in California. That was 1952. My family was here for a lot longer than that, and my grandparents were determined to buy close to where our family had settled, so they did."

"I see," she said, surprise leaking into her voice. The

statement was a revelation. First, Chinese Americans weren't allowed to own land until the 1950s? That was terrible—and shockingly recent. Second, he'd revealed they were in California. She *lived* in California—that much she knew. Did she live here, in the mountains? No…her home was somewhere farther away. That realization sent a tremor through her system, a warning that took her breath away. No more questions for now.

Despite Michael's warmth, the wind was chilling. *Trust him. Trust your path.* But it was getting harder to keep her frozen fingers locked onto Michael's coat. "Are we far?"

"Not far." His voice was frank, but there was concern, too. "After I put Dusty in the stable, we'll go straight into the greenhouse. If someone's been around there, we'll see their tracks."

Ellie closed her eyes and let out a sigh, trying to hold only the tiny kernel of hope that his reassurances lit, one that her fears could so easily snuff out. A tiny blessing.

When she opened her eyes, there was a break in the flurries and a wide-open valley spread out in front of her, covered with snow. Beyond the snaking river, through the trees, more of the ranch came into view. A smattering of log-cabin-style buildings, a barn and stable stretched along the riverside. The pastures were marked with a patchwork of wire fences and wooden posts. She spotted a few trucks parked at the far end of a large house and another one next to a smaller cabin. None of them white. The driveway snaked out of sight behind the hill. The place wasn't setting off alarm bells in her head, but all the open space made her uneasy. As the horse approached, she could see the stable was an older building, freshly painted red with new planks smoothly inserted between aging beams. Above the double doors hung a small plaque with an expertly carved symbol of a horse.

Ellie climbed down from Dusty gingerly, her icy feet stinging with each step. She brushed her hand along the carved details alongside the door. "Someone put their heart into restoring this building," she said half to herself. She glanced up at Michael. "It's beautiful."

Was that a trace of red flooding his high cheekbones? "I've done some work on it to turn it into a guest ranch. The place means a lot for my family."

She could have sworn she heard a note of regret in his voice.

"Are you selling?" she asked.

He shook his head. "My parents and grandparents are staying, but maintaining a working ranch is hard. The guest ranch means they can keep living here as they age."

There were emotions in his voice she couldn't identify and Ellie opened her mouth to ask more, but the openness she'd detected in his expression shuttered closed. It was none of her business.

Michael led Dusty into the stables, and she followed him as the warm, pungent scent of horses surrounded her. A wave of nostalgia hit her as a flash of memory came back: Mucking the narrow stall as she talked to Buster, a palomino. *Her* palomino. She tried to probe that memory, bring it into focus, but it faded behind the hazy veil in her mind, leaving her heart thumping. Why couldn't she remember?

Ellie wasn't sure how long she had been standing there, staring at the empty stall in front of her, but when she looked up, Michael was watching her.

"Ready?"

She knew that following him to a place with dry clothes

and food was her best option, but the unfamiliar property felt like a field full of land mines. She had no way to know which step would explode on her. Still, she followed him out into the unknown.

Michael trudged through the snow, toward the large, log-cabin-style house. The storm had let up a little, but new clouds were building to the west and coming in fast. Ellie's teeth were chattering uncontrollably, and her frozen feet felt like they'd shatter if she stepped too hard. They rounded the side of the house, finally out of sight of the driveway. The greenhouse was fairly large, not far from the back door of the house, and the windows were streaked with condensation. Michael kicked through the drifts that had gathered on the steps and opened the door.

Ellie stepped inside the little glass building. The air was warmer than outside and damp, imbued with the dank scent of soil. Much of the place was filled with long rows of raised beds in various stages of growth, and the ground was paved with stone. Along one wall was a kitchenette, with a stainless-steel counter and a sink, and in the middle there was a long, wooden table. Ellie hobbled over the bench next to the table and sank down on the one closest to the door.

"We keep the building warm enough so the pipes don't freeze, but it's not enough to warm you." Michael pulled a small heater out of one of the cabinets, plugged it in and set it next to her. Warm air rushed out, so warm, it made her want to cry. The cold had dulled her fear of attack, making her reckless with the need to get out of the storm. He passed her a small towel, and she wiped her face, smudging the cloth with makeup. Michael grabbed a tub from the cabinet under the sink then turned on the hot water tap, adjusting the temperature, testing it with the inside of his wrist.

As she watched him fill the tub, she probed experimentally at the bump on the back of her head. The area was still a little sticky, but it didn't seem to be bleeding anymore. Her headache had receded and the second bag of almonds seemed to be keeping the nausea at bay. Should she mention the injury to Michael? No. If she did, it would probably lead to more questions, questions she wasn't ready to answer yet.

"This is my grandma's way of warming us up," he said over his shoulder as he lifted the tub out of the sink. "It works faster than anything else I've tried."

"I'm willing to try anything," she said.

She cupped her hands and blew on them, then held them in front of the heater. Little bursts of heat stung her fingers, which she supposed was a good sign. At least they weren't numb.

Michael set the tub next to her feet on the floor. "Can you take off your boots by yourself?" he asked, his gaze on her hands.

"Of course," she said, but her fingers were stiff enough to make her wonder if she could.

Ellie reached down and untied the laces with shaky hands then pulled off one boot and the other. As she peeled off her socks, Michael slid the tub of warm water closer. She dipped her left foot in and winced as the warm water burned her frozen skin.

He frowned. "Too hot?"

She shook her head as the pain dulled and threads of warmth made their way up her legs. "Perfect."

She plunged her right foot in, winced again, then let out a sigh of relief.

"I'll bring back some warmer clothes from the house," he said.

"Won't they be missed?"

Michael shook his head. "We have extras. You okay alone for a few minutes?"

Alone. The word shuddered through her. She glanced around at the windows that surrounded her, but all she could see was snow. If someone came to the door right now...

"Isabel probably has some soup on the stove," he added.

Hunger warred with fear inside her. Ellie took a deep breath and tamped down the anxiety. "That would be wonderful. Thank you."

Michael nodded, exited, and disappeared into the house.

Ellie was definitely in trouble, and Michael hadn't the faintest clue what was wrong. If Ellie was even her name. She had sounded unsure of that most basic piece of information.

Her fashionable pants and thin leather boots looked both expensive and completely inappropriate for wandering in the mountains, so she likely hadn't planned to be out in the weather. His first guess had been domestic violence, sadly too common in the world. Maybe that was the case, but the more time he'd spent with her, the more he'd seen something extra: hints of confusion woven into her fear. This concerned him the most, the moments when she'd seemed to forget about everything and get lost in her thoughts. At times, she'd seemed eager to rid herself of his company, and as much as he respected that she was the best judge of her situation, he was still wary of turning her out on her own. Especially considering the incoming storm and the hungry animals that roamed the territory this time of the year. When she'd heard the sound of the truck coming down the road, the look she'd given him was a plea that had hit him straight in the gut. Even though he wasn't the right kind of man to answer pleas anymore.

But as Michael made his way down the hallway toward the kitchen, he was startled with another thought. On the ride down the mountain, into the stables and into the greenhouse, his focus on Ellie had pulled him from the depths of his grief. He'd felt a kind of purpose, a pull to action that he hadn't felt since before his life had crumbled.

The warm scent of some sort of chicken soup wafted out the doorway to the kitchen. Isabel Rodriguez stood by the counter, her hair pinned neatly off her face and plaited into a long braid down her back. She was scraping dough from the sides of the bowl of the standing mixer.

Before they'd hired Isabel, Michael's grandmother and his mother had alternated as head chefs of the ranch, but it had worn on them during the summers when the giant wooden dining table was packed with ranch hands. Now, with plans to expand, there was no way they could handle it all. Isabel had been a few years out of San Francisco Culinary Institute with an eclectic mix of prestigious restaurant experiences on her résumé. Her ties to the Tahoe area were strong, and she'd said in her interview that she'd been looking for a way to move to the region. His mother loved Isabel's experience in a high-end Chinese restaurant in San Francisco, and Michael liked her easygoing manner enough that she was one of the only people outside his family he regularly spoke with these days.

Isabel gave him a quick smile and set her spatula on the counter. "What's up?"

"I have a favor, and for right now it needs to stay between the two of us," he said then added, "That includes my parents."

Isabel looked at him with a seriousness that made him feel like she was reading this jumble of emotions that stirred inside him, maybe better than he was. She hadn't been there through Sunny's battle with cancer, but she seemed to understand the depths of his lowest moments.

"What's the favor?"

"Remember that argument my father heard this morning when he was out in the barn?"

She nodded, and a crease formed between her eyebrows.

"I found a woman by the line camp. She's scared and doesn't want anyone to know she's here. And there was a truck that stopped in front of our driveway…" Michael still wasn't sure about the truck. Was the driver lost, or was something more sinister at play?

Isabel frowned. "Do you suspect domestic abuse?"

"I don't know what to think."

Ellie was facing some sort of threat—that much he was sure of—but why had she said she didn't know? He hadn't gotten the sense she was lying… Michael blew out a breath. "She's soaking her feet in the tub, but a little soup would help her warm up."

"Of course." She grabbed a mug from the dishrack and ladled a steamy scoop. "What do I say to your father if he asks where you are?"

Michael couldn't bring himself to ask her to lie. "Tell him I'll give him the details later. The woman doesn't want anyone to know she's here."

She handed him the mug and a large bag of trail mix. "Let me know if you—"

"Did you hear that?" Michael could have sworn he'd just heard a cry. Ellie's cry.

Isabel shook her head. "Not sure what you're talking about…"

"Lock the door behind me."

Michael didn't hear her reply. He was already running out the door toward the greenhouse.

THREE

Ellie sat on the wooden bench, huddling over the tub of warm water, as she combed through the chain of events that had started in the cave, searching for something that would help her understand what was happening. How could she protect herself if she didn't know what she was running from?

Maybe it was just a coincidence that the people in the white truck had stopped in front of the Tang Ranch driveway. If it wasn't, who were they? The man who'd attacked her wouldn't have had time to get a truck and track her down so quickly…would he?

Ellie shivered. Something about being followed, being tracked, was ringing a bell, distant and muted, from behind that hazy veil in her mind.

You are safe, she told herself, but it didn't help. The greenhouse was designed to offer an unbroken view across the valley and the mountains, with floor-to-ceiling windows that opened out into the snowy landscape. And under any other circumstances, it would have felt idyllic to sit there, but right now, Ellie felt exposed despite the fogged panes. She craned her neck, checking the windows behind her. The driveway and the other buildings of the ranch were out of sight. All she could see through the streaks in the moisture and melting snow was the faint darkness of the forest and lots more snow.

The moment Michael had walked out of the little building, she'd had the urge to follow him, to get out of this glass box that put her on display. But where would she go? Inside, where people she didn't know would see her? One of those people could very well be the person who'd attacked her. No, she had to wait for Michael, to keep a low profile until she figured out who she was running from.

Ellie shifted for another visual sweep of the vast expanse of land behind her, but when she turned, her breath caught in her throat. Two figures moved from the direction of the corner of the house, the corner where she and Michael had come from. She jumped up and ran, barefooted, across the cold stones toward the door, trying to get a better look. She peered through the streaks on the glass. She couldn't make out the details, but one wore a navy blue coat with a black knit cap and black all-weather pants, and the other wore a gray jacket and pants with a black hat. Both men—their wide shoulders and narrow hips made her almost sure they were men—wore gators pulled up over their noses and mouths. They were following the path she and Michael had made through the snow, heading straight for the door to the greenhouse.

Ellie's heart pounded harder, threatening to jump out of her chest. *These could be people who work here*, she reasoned. Michael had said there were other people on the property.

"Don't get paranoid," she whispered to herself. "Just pretend you belong here."

But the intensity of the way both men stared at the greenhouse door—at her? Yes. She wasn't just being paranoid. These men were looking for her.

Ellie shuffled backward until she hit the bench. She stumbled, stubbing her toe on the tub. The water splashed out as she searched the little building for somewhere to hide. Before she could assess her options, the man in the blue jacket pulled open the door and charged in.

"Leave!" she yelled. "You're trespassing."

"Oh, we *are* leaving," grumbled the man in gray. "And you're coming with us."

Ellie scrambled around the table, hitting her shin on the opposite bench. Gray Jacket headed around the left side of the table and Blue Jacket went right.

"Michael," she gasped before a large gloved hand clamped over her mouth.

She sucked in a breath then jabbed her elbow at Blue Jacket. He dodged it, but his hand loosened from her mouth.

She heaved in a breath. "Mic—"

The man growled and the hand tightened over her mouth again. Ellie wriggled, lifted her legs and slipped out from under the man's grip. But the guy in the gray coat caught one of her legs, pulling it out from under her, and she tumbled back onto the assailant in the blue coat. She struggled and squirmed, but both men held her tight.

"I didn't agree to break into this house," Gray Jacket muttered. "Someone knows she's here. They'll look for her."

"It won't matter if we get out of here," the other man said. "Now."

Gray Jacket muttered something else, but whatever debate was being waged, he wasn't winning because they headed for the door. Her feet were bare and vulnerable. Even if she did escape, how could she run in the snow without boots? Ellie struggled and yelled muffled cries through the hand that was firmly clamped over her mouth. *Please hear me, Michael*. She managed to free one leg and aimed her foot between Gray Jacket's legs. Her kick connected.

"Oooff." Gray let out a groan and doubled over, swearing.

Adrenaline surged through her, giving her hope. Her legs were free, and she twisted, trying to escape, but the other man still had a firm grip on her, one hand on her mouth and the other across her chest.

"Grab her feet," Blue Jacket snapped. "Don't mess this up."

"He said this was an easy job," the other man growled.

"Just get the door."

Ellie sucked in breaths between the fingers of the man's gloves, trying not to hyperventilate. They were going to take her somewhere, and as soon as she left this greenhouse, her chances of getting away would dwindle.

Please.

"Put. Her. Down."

Her eyes darted to the door in time to see Michael charging through it.

Blue didn't let go, but his stance shifted, like he was on the defensive. "We are trying to get her the help she needs."

"Doesn't look like it to me." Michael's voice was cold as he continued across the greenhouse toward her.

The men glanced at each other before Blue said, "Elizabeth's husband passed away a few months ago, and since then, she hasn't been herself. She's in the middle of a mental breakdown, and her family is desperately trying to find her."

Fear jolted through Ellie like a live wire to her system and she sagged against the man in the navy coat. *Elizabeth. Her family.* The words rattled through her, shaking loose shards of memories from behind the heavy fog that hung over her brain. An image of her parents flared in her mind, both tired and sunburned, eating in silence at the dinner table. Next came Clint and Janice, her in-laws: Janice, with her ever-present frown of sour disapproval, next to Clint's hard, blank stare. Ellie had never been good enough for the Alexander family. The Alexander family? Aidan Alexander's face appeared before her, those piercing blue eyes, his sandy hair short and carefully combed, and the easy smile that never sat quite right with her. In her mind, he stood with his arms crossed, like he owned the room. The way he rested his hand on her shoulder long enough that she'd avoided getting into conversations alone with him from that first time it had happened onward.

Another sliver of a memory appeared. Aidan and Sean standing on the back deck of Aidan's mountain home, deep in a heated discussion. Sean. Her *husband.* That memory washed over her with a heaviness that pulled her under. Sean was gone.

She and Sean had built a life together, for better or for worse, in sickness and in health, 'til death do us part. Ellie had spoken those words with all her heart in a church filled with people she barely knew, but it had never once crossed her mind that the last part—death—would come so soon. Now Sean was dead and those vows felt like a warning. Another shard of memory sliced into her: that moment her legs gave out and she sank to the floor of the checkout lane of the grocery store, next to the rack of flashy magazines, when Aidan had called, informing her of the crash that had taken Sean's life. *Why this, God?* she had whispered over and over again.

But the sadness faded as bone-deep, paralyzing fear took over, closing in on her. Ellie's body shook as she tuned in to the words Gray Jacket spoke.

"We're worried she's a danger to herself. And probably to others."

Had she done something terrible? Every instinct inside Ellie shouted no, but she couldn't be sure of anything right now.

"Put her down and get off my property," said Michael, standing over her. "I'm only saying this once."

Michael's authoritative tone left no question that he would take action. He had been so careful with her, but now she could see another side of him, equally protective. This man was ready for anything.

Gray glanced at his partner in the navy coat. "I'm leaving," he finally said and hobbled toward the door.

Blue looked at Michael, his blue eyes wary over the gator mask. Then he dropped Ellie. She hit the floor, scrambled to her feet and watched, still stunned, as the men walked out the door.

"I'll be back," said Michael, turning away from her, heading for the door.

"No," she gasped. "Don't leave me alone."

Ellie hated how desperate she sounded, but she couldn't handle watching him walk away again.

Michael glanced at the men disappearing through the snow then swiped a hand over his face.

He turned to her. "These men came on my property, entered my house and attacked you. Men like this won't hesitate to come back, and the next time, they'll be better prepared. I need to find out who they are."

She couldn't let him go out, and not just for her own sake. For his sake, too.

"No. I'm leaving," she said. "You didn't ask for any of this, and now I'm putting your whole house in danger."

Michael saw a look of terror on Ellie's face. The men had said she was dangerous, but nothing about her suggested that.

Even now, just after she had been attacked, she was worried about the threat she'd bring to the rest of the household. This wasn't someone who posed a threat. But on the point of putting his whole house in danger—that, they agreed on.

He turned and watched as the men rounded the corner of the main house. He listened for the start of their car engine and waited until the sound of the engine faded. Then, fighting against every instinct, he forced himself to sit on the bench.

"Is any of what they said true?" he asked.

"The parts about my husband—his…death—that's true." Her throat bobbed as she seemed to swallow back emotion.

This woman had lost her spouse, too. Michael ignored the twist in his gut.

Then she added, "But the part about me being crazy? That's not true. At least, I don't think so."

She gave him the faintest of smiles. It was a beautiful smile; one that hinted at another version of this woman, confident, not afraid. Not bowing under fear and sorrow. His gut twisted again.

"The man called you Elizabeth. Is that what I should call you?"

She tilted her head, like she was considering the question. "It's what my husband and his family called me, but I prefer Ellie. That's what my parents called me when I was growing up."

As soon as the words left her mouth, she blinked, like the words she'd spoken had surprised her.

Michael frowned. There was something he was missing here. *Just help her the best you can.*

He glanced down at her bare feet then at the hip she was rubbing. "Are you hurt?"

She shrugged, rubbing the back of her head. "I have to

get out of here," she said quietly. "The next time they come back, it will be worse."

"Hold on," he said, ignoring the way his heart pounded at the urgency and fear in her voice. "You need to tell me what's going on."

He waited as the greenhouse grew quiet.

Ellie stared at him, as if she was assessing just how much to say. Finally, she let out a sigh. "That's the problem. I—I don't remember."

Michael quirked a brow. "What do you mean?"

"I woke up in a cave with a bump on my head, and all my memories are gone. When I came out, a man attacked me, but just when I had this feeling of recognition, my mind went...blank. I almost passed out. Something inside me didn't want to remember who he was." She shook her head again. "Even when you asked my name back on the mountain, I didn't know it until the moment I spoke. Then it just...came."

Michael blinked. The story sounded...well, a little far-fetched. Amnesia? Or maybe she was protecting herself, making something up that meant she didn't have to tell him more. But he'd seen that strange confusion and surprise in her expression when she'd said her name. And it made sense that she wouldn't want to see anyone if she didn't know who was after her—as much sense as any other explanation.

"It's really strange," she continued. "When we were in the stall, I remembered my horse, the one I had growing up."

"Do you remember anything else?"

She was quiet and a crease formed between her brows. Finally, she sighed. "It's like a handful of pictures in my mind. I can see my parents at the dinner table. I can taste my dad's chili, and I can hear my mother saying my name, but I can't see outside the edges of that picture."

"It's okay. It'll come," he said, though he had no idea if that was true. "Did you check your pockets for anything personal?"

"That was the first thing I did." She dug into her pockets and emptied the contents onto the table. The only thing that was close to personal was the car key. "I'm sure I have a phone. Why wouldn't I have it with me?"

Michael studied her carefully. "And what were you doing in that cave…?"

Her pink lips pulled down into a frown and her gray eyes looked lost. Then Ellie's eyes brightened, as if a piece of this strange puzzle had clicked into place.

"I knew the man who attacked me by the cave, but I didn't recognize anything about those other men." Her voice was filled with a mix of confusion and realization. "Which means neither of them was the person who attacked me outside the cave."

"Are you sure?"

"Positive. The first attack…the man's voice triggered this feeling, like my brain was shutting down. This time, I was terrified, but it wasn't the same. I didn't feel like I would pass out."

Michael was doing his best to trust her, but the story was hard to put together. "How would these men know to come around here?"

"They must have been in that white truck that stopped at the end of your driveway. Maybe the person from the cave told them the direction I went?"

Michael nodded. It was a long shot. Then again, his family owned all the land for miles in either direction. It wouldn't be hard to narrow down where she might go.

"They could have followed our tracks here," she added.

It was the only thing that made sense, but it seemed a

little extreme. Unless those men had a very strong incentive to find her and bring her back.

"So three men have tried to attack you, and you don't know why?"

Ellie closed her eyes. "They said they were going to take me somewhere."

Now she was watching him closely, as if she was gauging his reaction.

"You must think I'm a little...unbalanced," she added, shaking her head slowly. "Frankly, I'm thinking the same thing."

She looked behind him, out the windows, and he did the same. The snow was still coming down, and Michael wondered how long they had until the men returned. He was sure Ellie was thinking the same thing.

"I need to get out of here."

Michael nodded slowly. Her story definitely pushed the boundaries of believable, and yet those two men were very real and willing to drag her out of his house. What was he supposed to do with this?

Guide me, Lord.

The prayer flowed through his mind so naturally, the way prayer used to. And, for a moment, he zipped back to the time when it was a part of his life. When Sunny was a part of his life. Michael gave himself a little shake. This wasn't the time to probe his own past. He knew what he had to do. Deep down, he had known it from the moment she had come charging down the mountain. Even if Ellie was having some sort of mental health crisis and needed professional help, she also needed an ally now. He was going to be that person. He had to stay close until he was sure she felt safe.

"We should call the police," he suggested.

The moment he said it, she recoiled. "No police."

She looked like she was going to bolt. He glanced at her bare feet and put up his hands in surrender.

"No police," he repeated. "Can you tell me why?"

"I don't know." Her brow furrowed and she frowned. "Something about it scares me."

Was he going to trust her instincts? It was either that or leave her to fend for herself in the cold—which he definitely wasn't going to do. For now, he was going to trust her.

"I don't suppose you would know of a safe place I can take you?" he asked.

Her brow still wrinkled, she shook her head. "I—I don't think I live around here."

"But you're not sure where you live?"

She grimaced. "I think my best hope is to trace my path and try to figure out where I was before the cave. I kept this key." She picked up the key and stared at it in the palm of her hand. "It must lead to a car, and it can't be too far away from that cave where I woke up."

"You're planning to go on foot?"

"I'll be fine." She glanced at her bare feet then back at her boots, wilted into a soggy heap. "But I'd really appreciate a pair of boots to borrow."

There was no way Michael was sending her out into a blizzard on foot by herself when she had no idea who she was or where she was going.

"I can drive you around, see if you recognize anything."

She shook her head. "They were on the road, looking for me."

"What about a snowmobile? We can trace the path much quicker. Which means the tracks you left are less likely to be covered in snow."

She tilted her head to the side. "'We'?"

"Yes, *we*," he said firmly. "There's a storm outside, and I can't let you get lost on our property. You're stuck with me, at least until I'm sure you have a path to safety."

Ellie raised an eyebrow. "I'm not free to leave on my own right now?"

Michael sighed. "Of course you are. I…" He took a deep breath, searching for the right words. "I just feel strongly that you'd be much better off with a partner. For now."

And if she said no? He had no idea what he'd do.

She glowered and then glanced out the window again. "I want to be the one who decides what we do and where we go. Agreed?"

"Agreed."

The fear had receded from her gaze and all he saw now was determination. "Okay. We'll go together."

FOUR

Ellie clutched Michael's waist as the snowmobile's motor sawed and hummed under her. Wet snowflakes smacked the visor of her helmet as they traced their path back up the mountain. The horse's tracks were mostly buried in the snow and the forest was a blur of dark green around them. The blowing snow made it impossible to see much of anything.

Had she really planned to set out by herself on foot? Tracing her steps up the mountain in this weather would have been disastrous. She supposed that was what desperation did to a person. And that was what she'd felt in those moments after the second attack: desperate to escape the danger that could come from anywhere.

But now Ellie was grateful for the vehicle and the backpack under its seat, packed with food, a first-aid kit, and whatever else Michael had stuffed into it. And she was finally warm, thanks to the black shell jacket and pants, a muff that covered her neck, and a pair of sturdy work boots Michael had loaned her. She had tucked her hair into the helmet in front of the mirror, making sure all traces of her vibrant strands were covered. Maybe it would mean they could search for her car anonymously, or maybe there was other trouble waiting ahead for them—trouble she was pulling Michael into. *Michael.* Their paths were now connected.

Everything about him suggested he wanted to help her, and right now, Ellie didn't have a lot to go on beyond instinct. She had no choice but to trust him, at least for the moment.

The motor shifted as they approached the end of the driveway. Michael came to a stop on a low mound of snow left by the plow at the edge of the road. He shut off the engine. All that was left was the howl of the wind. Gusts raced down the hill, loud enough that they swallowed up everything else. Were her attackers lurking somewhere nearby? The two men from the greenhouse were strangers, so how was her family involved? That question roared like a flame, warning her away, and her life remained shrouded in an ominous cloud of smoke that lurked, threatening in her mind. Something terrible had happened and the clock was ticking. She had to figure out why she was running before her attackers found her again. Because they *would* find her—that much she was sure of.

Michael pointed down the road where new tire tracks lay barely covered in the snow. There were footprints on the road, leading directly to the path they were on.

"Looks like someone's been here recently, checking our path," he said through the intercom in the helmet.

"Our tracks are still visible." If anything, the snow hid the fact that it was a horse and not human track.

Michael gave a little nod, and then the engine sputtered to life again. They crossed the road and started up along the switchbacks. On the steeper patches, the tall pines gave way to exposed jumbles of granite. She had been too frightened to pay attention to the path on their ride down the mountain, to landmarks they'd passed. The whole sequence from when she'd been attacked outside the cave to the moment she'd tugged on the thick socks Michael had brought from the house for her was all a blur. But now, as they retraced their steps, Ellie could see they'd traveled much too far to go on foot, especially in the snow. Plus, the higher they got in elevation, the more the clouds obscured the view.

Thank you, Lord, for leading me to Michael. If He hadn't, she'd likely have frozen to death out here.

The motor revved around one corner then the next and the next, until they were in front of the cabin where she'd found Michael. The snowmobile came to a stop right where he'd picked her up.

She studied the dark cabin and her first thought sent a spike of panic through her. "Does anyone live here?"

Michael shook his head. "Especially not in the winter. No water, no electricity. It's just a line camp."

Just. Yet something in his voice told her it meant more to him. She waited for Michael to continue, but he was quiet. It wasn't her business. Also, judging from what she knew of him, which was admittedly very little, Michael didn't seem like the type who did a lot of talking about himself. Or a lot of talking in general. In her current situation, that was ideal. Still, it felt strange that he had seen her in such a vulnerable place when she knew next to nothing about him.

"You came down the mountain from that direction," he said, pointing up at the hillside. "Recognize anything?"

She scanned the mountainside, straining to see through the snow. It all looked…white. With pine trees. Not helpful.

"I don't remember," she said. "I was in some sort of cave, and it was surrounded by big boulders."

"That doesn't really narrow it down. The mountain is full of boulders and caves."

"Maybe if we start up that way, I'll recognize something?" She could hear she sounded just as uncertain as she felt.

"There's another road about a mile up, in that direction, too. Maybe the car is parked somewhere along there?"

She thought back to that flash of memory at Aidan's house, the one that looked out at the mountains. Was her car parked at his place? The idea sent a jolt of fear through her, but it didn't shake loose any more memories.

"What's up there?" she asked.

"It's a newer development. I have no idea how they got that one past the environmental commission, considering it's located right in avalanche territory—"

Ellie's body went rigid with fear. *Environmental commission.*

Michael must have noticed the way she clung to him. He put his hand over hers and turned around. She couldn't read his eyes through the visor, and she was glad he couldn't see the fear on her face.

"What did I say?" His voice was gentle.

"I—I don't know," she finally said. "Something about avalanches and the environmental commission—that was familiar." And not in a good way. "But I don't remember anything more. Finish what you were saying."

Michael gave her a wary look then nodded. "My father and my grandfather went to the city council meetings to protest, but the builders promised to be responsible land stewards. They even bought extra parcels and donated them as parkland." A vague sense of foreboding grew inside her as he spoke, shaking his head. "Now that the trees are gone and the hillside is all dug up, there's nothing to do about it. They paid their fines, but we're all going to pay the price of the unstable mountain face."

Ellie shivered. Somehow, she was connected to this. She was sure of it.

"You want to continue?"

"Definitely." Dread told her she was getting closer to the truth about herself, her life, and that none of these problems would go away until she knew what was going on. She needed to go forward, to follow the fear and uncover whatever her brain was hiding from her. There must be reasons she couldn't remember, and the way her whole body wanted to shut down each time she came close to remembering something suggested she shouldn't push this. But she had no choice, not if she didn't want to find herself cornered again. She needed to trust that God would help guide her.

Michael started the engine again and headed in the direction she'd come on her way down the slope earlier. They were off the trail now, moving slowly as they climbed through the trees. The wind died as they moved through the mist of the clouds. Ellie searched for something familiar as they wound through boulders and stands of pines, but all she saw was more snow. Wisps of cold found their way through the sleeves of her jacket and along her back as they traveled through the forest.

Michael slowed as they passed a jumble of boulders jutting out of the snow. "Does this look familiar?"

She scanned the veiled landscape, waiting for that jolt of recognition. It didn't come.

"I don't think so."

"We'll keep going."

The snowmobile continued up the mountain, passing stands of tall trees and snowy ledges. Michael slowed at each outcropping of rock, but they all looked the same. The trees disappeared as they climbed above the misty clouds, revealing steep, rocky peaks with pockets of snow clinging to their sides. Ellie's heart sped up. She knew this place, but no memories came.

Michael ascended a steep incline and stopped at the top of a snowbank left by a season's worth of plows. Below was the road, two lanes, well-traveled, even in the blizzard. On the other side, the mountain continued, bare, with rock and soil clinging precariously to the face. They had climbed high enough to where the snow was measured in feet not inches. It was where the clouds hit the peaks and released everything they had, smothering the landscape. There was nothing familiar here, nothing that sparked a memory, so why was her heart pounding?

"We're getting closer. I can feel it," she said, forcing her voice to steady. "Where are we?"

He gestured to the right. "That direction leads toward a ski resort and, if you keep going, you'll hit town," he said. Then he pointed to the left. "Around that curve is the new development I was talking about."

Every instinct told her to turn back, to head downhill, far away from the direction Michael was pointing now. Ellie swallowed back the dread that was creeping up her throat. "The new development. That's where we need to go."

"What do you think about taking the road?" he asked, indicating the packed snow at the bottom of the bank. "No one knows we're on a snowmobile, and you're not identifiable in those clothes. There's no reason anyone would recognize you if we passed him."

That was true. And if she was going to find her car, they needed to follow the road. Still, driving out in the open felt like a really bad idea. So did going toward the new development.

Trust Michael, she told herself. She needed to trust that they could navigate whatever came next.

"Let's do it," she said.

"Speak up the moment you see anything familiar."

The snowmobile engine sputtered as Michael maneuvered them down the snowbank. Fresh tire tracks marked the road in both directions and, as they rounded a corner, a fancy red Jeep bumped past in the opposite direction, setting her heart racing.

Calm down. Focus.

As the first mailbox came into view, her heart took off again. She knew this place. It wasn't her home but—

"Anything?"

"It's familiar. We're definitely going the right direction." She was panting she realized as she tried to slow her breaths. "What's the plan if we see the truck that stopped in front of your ranch?" The truck almost certainly belonged to the two men who'd attacked her. "If I'm familiar with the area, someone is likely looking for me here."

"We'll go off-road as soon as there's an opening. This area used to belong to another rancher before he sold, so I can navigate the mountain."

That eased the building fear a little.

Michael slowed further as they passed another driveway, but she could barely make out the shape of the house through the snow. She peered down the next driveway and caught a glimpse of the front corner of a white truck.

She gasped into the intercom.

"I saw it, too," said Michael. "Should we turn back?"

"Maybe it's a coincidence," she said, swallowing her fear. "Let's see if it follows us."

They continued forward and, after they passed the next mailbox, Ellie forced herself to focus on the road in front of her. That's when she saw it. A silver SUV smashed against the snowbank of someone's driveway, covered in snow.

My car.

"That's it!" she cried through the microphone.

Michael pulled up next to the Cadillac and slowed to a stop as her memories came crashing in…

The business meeting of the three owners of Green Living

Construction: Aidan, his father, Clint, and Ellie. Her refusal to approve the next stage of the company's new Pine Ridge development until she read over the entire environmental report herself. As an accountant, she'd been coming at it from a financial perspective, but the moment she had refused to sign, she'd known she was on the trail of something. Then there was the glare of open bitterness from Clint when he'd said, *You have no right to Sean's part of this business. You haven't heard the last of this.* The warning Aidan had given her after he'd followed her out to the parking lot and stared her down with cold eyes, crowding her against her car door. *Leave the business decisions to me and live your life as you did before, or your life will never be the same. We'll never leave you alone. We'll ruin your life, just like you want to ruin ours.*

Someone had appeared on her tail as she'd driven back to the cabin. *She had a cabin?* A vision of the place came back, an enormous wooden house along a row of near-identical houses. It was so much bigger than the one she'd grown up in, and it wasn't even their primary residence. But someone had followed her, inching closer and closer. She had taken a different route, so how had they found her? And then… Nothing. The memories ended there.

Ellie climbed off the snowmobile. The desire to keep this connection to her memories, this lifeline to herself, was strong enough to make her knees wobble. *Am I having a mental breakdown? Is any of this real?* There was one way to find out. She reached into her jacket pocket and pulled out the key fob. This would tell her whether her recollections were real. She pressed it, and the car beeped as the doors unlocked.

"That's my car," she whispered as glimmers of the past reeled through her mind. "I know what happened—"

But before she could finish her sentence, a motor revved behind her and she caught a flash of metal out of the corner of her eye. When she turned around, the white truck they'd seen earlier was roaring straight for them.

Michael did a double-take as the white truck skidded straight for them. They were at the center of something, and Michael had no idea what it was. All he knew was that he had to get Ellie out of there.

"Get on!" he shouted, grabbing the sleeve of her jacket.

She froze and, for one long moment, he wasn't sure if she'd come. *Help her.* But she came to life and leaped onto the back of the snowmobile, her arms tightening around him.

He gunned the motor just as the truck swiped the corner of the buried silver Cadillac, right where Ellie had been standing seconds ago. He glanced over his shoulder and caught a glimpse of the truck fishtailing. Michael took off down the narrow road, the snowbanks rising up on both sides. The snowmobile was old, better suited for winter inspections of their ranch property, not for outrunning trucks on the street. But he was grateful for what they had as he took the curve hard. Now he just needed to find a way off the road. Ellie leaned into him as the snowmobile sputtered then shot forward.

Protect Ellie.

The instinct ran through him, bone-deep, as he steered the vehicle into the wintry landscape. Visibility was low, especially around the curves, and if any trees or power lines were down… He'd figure that out when it happened.

The handles vibrated under his gloves. He tightened his grip.

"How far is the truck?"

She shifted behind him. "Maybe twenty yards away?"

Too close. They had to get off the street, but the snow-banks that lined the road were too high to safely climb at anything faster than a crawl. He could turn off onto one of the driveways, but that would mean leading a car chase right to someone's home. It could be a dead end—or, worse, what if the owner of the house was outside, shoveling their driveway? Then one more person would be in harm's way. No, he couldn't risk it.

"We need to get off the road," he muttered. "Somewhere past this development where a truck can't go. I need an exit."

He'd said it to more to himself, but Ellie answered. "What about the driveway into the national forest, farther ahead on the left? They plow the parking lot, so there will be a break in the snowbank, but the recent snowfall might make it too deep for them to follow us easily."

Her words sent a little jolt through his system. She knew where she was. *She remembered.* He had a load of questions for her, but right now wasn't the time. Instead, he weighed her suggestion. It might work, as long as they could keep the white truck at a distance. As long as they made it through this development.

"Good idea. We'll try it." He revved the engine. The moun-tainside was too bare, exposing the oversize houses, The snowmobile slid around the next curve and the engine sput-tered as it grasped at the snow underneath it. They rounded another curve, drifting precariously into the opposite lane.

"How far are they now?" he asked.

"Closer, but their truck is skidding on the snow."

Michael doubted that would get them to slow down. In-stead, it made the truck more dangerous. If the driver lost control, would the vehicle come skidding toward them?

As they raced past a wide driveway, Ellie's voice came

through the intercom. "That's the last house in the development. The national park is just around the next bend."

"The turn will be tight, so I'll need to slow down." That meant the truck would get closer.

"I'm ready." She tightened her grip around his waist and another rush of warmth spread through him.

Please, God, give me the courage and the sense to pull this off. For Ellie.

Michael hugged the next curve, trying to gain some distance on the large white truck. "How close are they?"

"Maybe ten yards."

Too close.

The break in the wall of snow came into view. The more recent snowplowing had blocked the entrance for a truck, but their sled would be fine as long as he took time to get over it—time he didn't have. He had to pull this off fast. That meant there was no room for error.

"We are putting ourselves in your hands, God," he breathed.

These were words he never thought he'd say again. Not after God had taken Sunny away from him. Michael's anger at God, at the unfair world around them, still lived inside him. His faith had been shaken, but somehow it was still alive. Somehow, the words came out.

"Amen," said Ellie.

"Here we go."

He scanned for oncoming traffic then gunned the motor, hugging the right snowbank. When they were just a few yards away from the road into the park, he slammed on the brakes then turned to the left. The snowmobile skidded through the snow, turning until the sled was pointing toward the crossroad. But they hit ice, slick and uneven, and the snowmobile slid and bumped past it. The engine sputtered as the track grabbed for the snow.

Out of the corner of his eye, Michael could see the white truck speeding toward them. *Focus.* Michael fixed his gaze on the opening in the snowbank and throttled the motor. The engine stammered then jolted forward. The truck was only a few yards away, and it swerved, moving far too fast for control on the ice below it. As the snowmobile started onto the heap of drift, the truck's bumper clipped their back ski, jolting them sideways, pulling them back. The truck swung around, its side sliding straight for them. Michael revved the motor again and they took off up the snowbank, leaping through the air just before the side of the vehicle slammed into them. Ellie clung to him as they flew into the deep snow and landed with a hard jolt.

"You okay?" he yelled.

"Yes. *Go.*"

Michael's heart jumped in his chest as they raced along the deserted winter drive. He took a couple deep breaths. "Can you see them?"

Ellie shifted behind him. "They're right there at the entrance, but I think they're stuck."

"Good," he said, driving them deeper into the park. He continued until he found a break in the wall along the side of the road. It looked like a ski trail, but it hadn't been used in a while.

He drove up the mound and followed the trail into the forest, trying to get his breathing under control. The trail wove through the forest and then forked. Michael brought the sled to a stop at the fork and turned off the motor. The forest was quiet, but his heart was still jumping, his ears ringing from the buzz of the snowmobile's engine.

Thank you, God, for showing us the way.

He was sweating and his arms ached from grasping the handles of the snowmobile. He flexed his hands then climbed off the vehicle. He waded through the deep snow, trying to process what had just happened. Michael laced his hands behind his head and took a couple of long, slow breaths. There was no mistake. The men in that vehicle had wanted to get them badly enough to risk injuring everyone, themselves included.

He and Ellie were still alive. He had kept her safe. He had done it. Relief poured through him, so intense that his breath caught in his throat. He had failed Sunny, but he had not failed Ellie—not yet. That meant something. If he could be there for Ellie right now, maybe he could get out from the heaviness that clouded every morning, every night, even his dreams. Maybe. After all, he had found himself praying when faith had escaped him for years.

But the burst of hope was chased with a twist of guilt. How had he connected Ellie and Sunny so easily in his mind? Sunny had been his soul mate, his perfect match, and he hardly knew Ellie. Michael pushed away the messy thoughts. They were in the middle of a forest buried in snow, and a truck had just tried to run them off the road—a truck almost certainly driven by two men who had already tried to kidnap Ellie. And those two men weren't the only ones after her. They were nowhere near safe yet.

Finally, he turned to Ellie. She had taken off her helmet and was scanning the forest with a dazed look in her eyes, like she was just as shaken up as he was. Her fiery hair was tamped down from the helmet, but when she shook her head, her curls sprang back to life.

Michael took off his helmet and looked into her gray eyes, wide and serious.

"Thank you," she said.

Michael's breath caught at the ring of her voice in the still winter forest, so full of gratitude and a hint of awe.

"You're welcome." He swallowed, forcing him to focus on the urgency of the situation, not the way his heartbeat sped up when she met his eyes. "Tell me what's going on. Everything you remember."

FIVE

Ellie's breaths came quickly, one after another, as her brain rattled through memory after memory, fear after fear. Sean's family was behind all of this. They had sent two men in search of her. How many more were out there? And then there was this: she had just put Michael's life in danger. Michael, who had trusted her story, no matter how outrageous it sounded. Who had stayed with her instead of letting her go into the storm alone. In return, she had put him in danger. She needed to convince him to go separate ways before that happened again. That meant she needed to get at what was waiting for her at the cabin and then disappear as soon as possible.

But first, Michael wanted answers. He deserved them. Where did she start with the string of memories that bombarded her as she tried to follow one after another?

Without the helmet's visor, the snow glowed bright white against the gray clouds that enveloped the mountain. Michael had taken off his helmet, too, and that unwavering gaze was focused solely on her. Warmth spread through her. His eyes were so dark and serious, and yet, up close, she could see fine lines that fanned from the corners. Laugh lines, despite the heaviness he carried. How long had it been since he'd laughed? Loss had changed him, just as it had her. The connection brought a closeness as he gazed intensely at her. What she would have given for Sean to look at her like that in those last months. Instead, he had closed himself off. The thought caught her off guard, strong and so…disloyal. Ellie quickly pushed it away and focused on what to tell Michael, where to start.

"I saw the car, and memories came back," she said. "It's a lot."

Michael's expression softened. "I'd say take it slowly, but we're not in that position right now."

Ellie took a long breath. "When my husband, Sean, died, everything went to me, including his third of the family's real estate development business. At first, I was too shocked to register what part-ownership meant, but as I started to get his affairs in order, I read up on everything. To be a responsible owner. I mean, how could I be an owner if I wasn't involved?"

Michael nodded. She thought that sounded reasonable, but Aidan and Clint hadn't.

"The company buys up land and builds houses, upscale houses, on it. They built all the houses we just passed." She gestured in the direction of the development they'd driven by moments before.

The next part was the hardest to speak aloud and another rush of discomfort flooded her. It felt disloyal to talk about any of this. But her danger was his right now. He needed to know.

"Aidan and Sean had some sort of argument about regulations. I don't know exactly what happened, but from what I could tell in the emails, they paid a small fine for environmental violations but still made record profits. And then there were other payments to two of the city council members that looked a lot like bribes." She closed her eyes. "I don't know if the evidence is enough to hold up in court. But my husband was one of those people you were talking about before. One of the people who came in, breaking laws and ignoring the environmental regulations." She swallowed and added, "I'm sorry."

Michael looked at her with those serious eyes. "You're not responsible for the choices he made."

A gust of wind blew through the forest, sweeping her hair across her face and making her shiver. But Michael didn't seem to notice the cold or the snow. He was focused solely on her.

Ellie tucked the stray curls behind her ear and continued. "I dug further and found some environmental reports from the development we drove through. I didn't know what to do."

She frowned. "Then Aidan and my father-in-law, Clint, called a meeting to get me to sign off the paperwork for a contractor in a new development. But when I brought up the emails I'd found, they both turned angry. Enough that I walked out of the meeting.

"I made the mistake of telling them my thinking." She took another deep breath as embarrassment flooded through her. "Not a good move, but I guess I just couldn't quite believe that they were up to something underhanded. Because that meant…" This was the hardest part. She swallowed and pushed herself to say her worst fears aloud. "That meant that Sean was probably involved, too."

This was the dread that had been sitting in her, lurking, the darkness that had consumed her. "Someone followed me home and, the moment I realized it, I must have swerved into the snowbank…"

The fear, the car crash, the bump on her head she couldn't even remember—all of that had a role in this feeling that the ground had shaken below her, toppling her life with Sean, which had seemed so solid, so steady. *Is this the man I married?* It was another layer of dread hiding in those memories of the crash—one she could feel, buried deep inside—and as she spoke, this fear stirred, threatening to awaken. It was fear that her whole life with Sean, the love she'd thought they shared, wasn't real. Had she loved a man who had pulled off harmful things right under her nose?

Ellie had tried so hard to live a life that her parents could be proud of. Her parents had worked hard on their ranch, but it hadn't seemed to matter. It was a dying way of life, taken over by big farms and the grab for land to extend the never-ending suburban sprawl. But they had hung on, tooth and nail, scraping by and saving to make sure she could go to college. And she'd studied, never forgetting how much was riding on her success. Still, college would have remained out of reach without the grants and scholarships she had gotten, both from her little town and from the State of California.

So it was both a source of pleasure and a touch of embarrassment when she'd found out how easily money flowed in the Alexander family. She'd never told her parents all the details, though they must have suspected when they'd showed up for the lavish wedding Sean's mother had insisted on. Still, she'd believed that Sean was a good man, an honest man. How could he have broken her trust like this?

She studied Michael's expression for censure, but she didn't find any. "Was he involved?"

"I don't know," she said quietly. That was the hardest part—suspecting but not knowing. "We didn't get far in the conversation because, as soon as I asked to see the full financial records, the tone of the meeting flipped. They refused, so I wouldn't sign off on the contract for the next phase of the project."

She shivered as the scene played in her mind. "Aidan followed me out to my car and told me that if I didn't let this go, he wouldn't leave me alone."

Michael's expression hardened.

"I needed to know if Sean was involved. So I headed back home, to search Sean's office for some sort of proof, one way or another." She shook her head. "I can see what a bad move that was now. I mean, both of them were outright hostile. What did I think would happen? But I just…couldn't let it go."

"We don't always make the best choices when so much is on the line," Michael said quietly, and she could feel that there were layers to that comment, a depth to it, and for a moment, a haunted look crossed his face. Yet the look disappeared almost immediately. "Who followed you home?"

"I'm not sure. I didn't go straight home, so I'm not sure how they knew exactly where I was. I have this feeling that I *do* know who followed me, somewhere inside. But after my car crashed into the snowbank… Everything after that is still gone."

"You need to go to the police," he said. "I'll drive you there. Right now."

She shook her head. "Aidan and Clint have almost certainly already talked to the authorities. You don't know what those men can be like. They're both really charming, friends with everyone, including half the police force. And they think they have a right to what they want." She closed her eyes. "I wish I could trust calling the police right now, but I can't take the risk. Not now, after I saw how they turned on me."

She was trying so hard not to panic. She had to focus on the next move, the path to safety.

"Sean left what he called a 'go bag' for me," she added. It was that last piece that was so damning. Why would she need survival supplies unless he had known that something was wrong?

Just in case, Sean had said. Looking back, it had happened a few days after the fight he and Aidan had had on the back porch. But the go bag was supposed to be for the two of them, for a quick departure. How long had he suspected they might need it?

"How could he say he loved me when he kept something this big from me?" she whispered. He must have known the danger he was putting them in.

She closed her eyes as the grief overwhelmed her. Sean had known something was wrong and he'd died without telling her what it was. What she wouldn't give to talk to him, to argue, to demand an explanation. Or even just to see him again. It was too much, and she fought to keep the tears inside. Now wasn't the time.

When she opened her eyes, Michael was crouching in front of her in the snow. His brown eyes were filled with so much compassion.

"I'm sorry this is happening to you," he said.

Ellie wasn't so sure she deserved his compassion. "It was my husband's company that leveled the trees and destabilized the mountain. And now it's my company, at least a third of it. You should be angry with me."

Michael shook his head. "I'm not. You didn't know. And it sounds like you were trying to make sure something like this didn't happen again."

"I can't believe Sean did this," she said quietly. "If he loved me…"

"No, Ellie. Don't go down that path. If you thought he loved you when he was alive, hold on to that feeling."

She took a long breath. Could she accept that she may never know Sean's reasons? It all came down to belief. Could she trust her experience, that their life together was truly filled with love?

The snowfall had eased in the little valley where they stood, and the forest was silent. Thick wet flakes lay everywhere, on her jacket, in Michael's hair. She looked at the man in front of her, reminding herself how good God had been to her despite everything. He had brought Michael into her life when she'd needed someone to trust.

Michael's eyes were so warm and caring, his face so handsome and rugged, and her heart thumped in her chest. His gaze was steady on her, and something strong, something big, passed between them. She swallowed. Grateful—that's what this feeling was, she told herself. She was grateful that he'd listened and hadn't judged... Or was this attraction?

A thunderous rumble echoed down the mountain, jolting her back to the present. It sounded like a cannon that wouldn't stop.

"Avalanche," said Michael. "Not close, thank God. But we need to get out of here."

She knew he wasn't going to like what she was about to say next. "I need that go bag. I need to go to my house for it."

Michael shook his head. "You know that's not safe."

"It's the only way," she said. "I need to disappear."

"If it's money you need, I can help you work that out," he said.

She shook her head and tried for levity. "Do you offer money to everyone who shows up on your property?"

The hint of a smile told her the answer might be yes, but he said, "Only the people with no memories."

Ellie found herself smiling. He was a good man, with such a generous offer. All the more reason not to get him involved in whatever was going on—any more involved.

"All I need is to be dropped off near the property."

"Drop you off?" He gave a humorless laugh. "Not a chance."

"I get to decide where I go, remember?" she said. "I'm going back to my house."

Michael couldn't believe what he was hearing. Ellie wanted him to drop her off at her house? She may as well have asked him to paint a target on her back, too. Helping Ellie run from danger was an easy choice, but helping her run toward it? That stirred up emotions he had buried years ago, emotions he had no interest in uncovering.

Except this whole situation wasn't about him or what he wanted. It was about what she needed. And he needed to keep his emotions out of this entirely.

Reluctantly, Michael admitted to himself that even if he didn't agree with her next move, he understood it. He looked into her eyes and saw steely determination. He admired this, that in a day full of more danger and fear than most people faced in their lifetime, she was determined, not defeated. He needed to accept the risks she was willing to take.

"And what happens if someone is waiting for you there?" he asked.

"Obviously, I won't go in if anyone is there. But I need to try."

He swiped a hand over his face. "How can you ask me to leave you alone at your house in a snowstorm?"

"I have an escape plan." Michael lifted an eyebrow and she added, "A good one, I promise."

"I want to stay with you until I see that plan in action."

She tilted her head to the side, like she was studying him.

"Your choice," she finally said. Then her expression softened. "We'll check the property for footprints and car tracks first."

Michael frowned. "I don't like this."

"Noted."

He gave a wry laugh and a hint of a smile twitched at the corners of Ellie's mouth. Then she sighed. "I don't like it either. What else am I supposed to do? Keep running with no money, no ID, nothing? Where does that take me?"

His family had helped many people over the years, whether it was his cousin who'd needed a little time away from city life or a woman who had wandered onto their property, hungry and with nowhere to go. Growing up, his father had offered support to more people than he could count, enough that Tang Ranch was known for generosity all the way back to the San Francisco Bay Area, where his aunties and uncles and cousins lived. And yet, help had never felt like *this*. Michael didn't want to think further about what *this* was, blooming inside him.

He opened his mouth to tell Ellie that he'd figure out how to help her, but she shook her head, like she could hear his thoughts. "No offense, but I need to be able to keep myself safe. On my own."

"Then we better get up there right away," he said. "Before the people in that truck dig themselves out of the snowbank. And let's hope they don't have cell service."

She nodded. "It's spotty over there, but no guarantees."

Michael's mind was at work, calculating their odds. Even if the men were working with the Alexander family and had made contact with one of them, they wouldn't know Ellie's exact location right now...though the snowmobile made enough noise to figure it out. He listened for others in the area, possible decoys, but there was only the wind. If someone wasn't already at the house, they'd need to get in and out of it fast enough to stay ahead of their pursuers.

He climbed onto the snowmobile again and pulled on his helmet. "Ready?"

"Yes." She put on her helmet and slipped her arms around his waist. He started the motor and, as he moved forward, her voice came through the intercom again. "Thank you. For believing me. For listening to me."

"You're welcome," he said as another rush of warmth spread through him.

It had been so long since he'd felt alive like this. The danger was part of it, but there was something more, a connection with Ellie. *It feels good to be helping someone else again*, he told himself as the snowmobile started over the wintry terrain. That was all this was. *Don't overthink it.*

Michael stayed lower on the mountain as they made their way over the bumpy terrain of the park toward private land. The mountain dipped into a valley then over a ridge. The forest ended as they crested the ridge, exposing the bare rocky land of the new development.

The Gibson family had once owned the strip of mountain between the park and Tang Ranch, but that was before ranching had gotten too hard and they'd needed to cash out. Michael hadn't faulted the family—they'd needed the money to start a new life for themselves—but Michael didn't like the fact that selling had been their only good option. Pete Gibson had apologized to the Tangs one night, just after Christmas, not long after he'd signed the deal. He'd told the family that the developers had promised to work with the community. But as soon as the snow had cleared that spring, the builders clear-cut all the trees on the mountainside—for fire safety, they'd said. And while this was true, there were other ways to avoid the forest fires that swept through the Sierra Nevada too often these days. First and foremost, not building right in the middle of forestland.

Once the trees were gone, there was nothing to be done about it, no matter how many codes they'd violated. Now the whole area was at a higher risk for avalanches in the snow and landslides in the rain.

Michael understood why Ellie would be stunned and hurt to find out her husband had been a part of that under-handed move—and then hidden it from her. But hearing more about what had happened with Sean's family, Michael wondered if there wasn't more to the story.

He turned the snowmobile up the mountain. They passed a sheer face of granite and a house came into view. They were now directly under the development.

"Which one is yours?" he asked through the intercom.

"The third one in on this side of the street." She paused. "What are the chances someone is waiting for us?"

"I've been trying to figure that out." He sounded worried. "We'll circle the area first to make sure."

He steered them farther up the mountain at an angle until they were riding just below the bushes and trees that marked the edge of the properties. They passed one enormous house then another. Each one seemed to be a variation on a theme: an oversize blend of traditional wooden cabins often seen in this area but with more grandiose sensibilities. The backs of the houses were lined with windows that towered up two stories and looked out over the mountain.

"These places must cost a fortune to heat," he said.

"They do. And when the power goes out and the generator is on, it's twice as much," she said. "Green Living Construction was having trouble selling these houses at first, so Sean and I took this one over informally. Just so more of the houses looked occupied, Sean said. It's technically still owned by the company, which means Aidan and Clint can sell it out from under me at any time. I think that's why they thought I'd be more cooperative—so I could reap the benefits of the arrangement."

"You think both Aidan and Clint would agree to do that?"

Ellie gave a humorless laugh. "They'd probably sell it tomorrow if there weren't still two more lots for sale." She sighed softly before admitting, "The place was too big for just two of us, and now it's ridiculous for just me."

"Are you ready to let the house go?"

"I guess I am," she said quietly, though he heard hesitation in her voice. Maybe she felt the same push and pull with the reminders of her past, too.

Michael slowed the snowmobile as they approached the back of the third house. He steered through the low trees then cut the motor. The embellished A-frame rose up out of the mountain, all wood and windows. The inside was dark, as far as he could see, and an untouched blanket of snow lay between them and an enormous deck that lined the back of the house and shot out into the yard. A motor droned in the distance, but it wasn't close.

Behind him, Ellie shifted, first in one direction then the other.

"Any signs of life?" he asked.

"Nothing yet."

"I'll circle the perimeter."

Michael started the snowmobile again and they puttered past the enormous deck, where the snow lay on the railing in towering white mounds. He pulled along the side. At one time, the trees would have separated one yard from another, but the newly planted saplings just barely poked through the feet of snow. It was bare, with each house looking into the next. They slowly moved into the front. Michael continued across the yard, out toward the street. He pulled up next to the bank left by the snowplow and came to a stop. Over the top, he could just barely see a long stretch of the road, snow-covered and empty in both directions.

"I see tracks in the driveway," said Ellie.

Michael drove along the snowbank up to the driveway to get a better look. Below the bank from the plow, there was a layer of new snow interrupted by a fresh set of thick tire tracks.

Footprints came out from both sides of the cab of the truck. One set led to the front of the house and another ventured into the deeper snow, leading to the far side of the house. Two people had been there, checking out the place.

"The men in that white truck," she said softly into the intercom. "You think it was them?"

"Let's hope so," said Michael. "Otherwise we have more problems on the way."

"Both Aidan and Clint have access to a set of keys since the company still owns the place," she said. "We never bothered changing the locks. But they don't have the code to the alarm."

The alarm wasn't going off, so it was likely no one was inside. Yet.

Ellie motioned to the far side of the house, next to the garage, and he followed that route. As they rounded the corner, a snow-covered mound came into view.

"This is my escape plan," she said, pointing at it. "There's a snowmobile somewhere under there."

"Do you have the keys?"

"We keep a set to everything in a lockbox next to the back door," she said. "I drove it into town a few weeks ago, after the last storm. It's gassed up, so all I need to do is pull off the cover." She patted him on his arm. "Satisfied with my plan?"

It was, in fact, a good plan, though he didn't feel any more comfortable leaving her on her own.

"Yes, I'm satisfied. But I don't want to leave until you have the money and your ID in your hand and I watch you drive away."

"Got it," she said, but there was a softness in her voice. Then she blew out a breath. "Pull up in back, and let's do this."

SIX

Ellie fumbled with the keypad, her bare fingers stiff from the cold. The roof of the porch sheltered the entryway from the brunt of the snow that covered the rest of the deck, but drifts had blown in during the storm, leaving almost a foot of powder under her feet. She'd shoveled after each storm this winter, but there was easily three feet of wet snow currently weighing down the deck. Michael stood behind her, listening, watching the hillside for movement. The snow had mostly let up, just tiny flakes drifting down, but to the west, dark billows of clouds hung low, heading straight for them. She usually loved this calm as a storm rolled in, but today the quiet was ominous. Every noise, every gust of wind, every distant hum of a motor put her on high alert. Someone would return here looking for her. It was just a question of when.

The lockbox sprang open and Ellie grabbed the set of keys. She inserted the correct one into the back door and pulled it open. She stepped in and quickly keyed off the alarm, gesturing for Michael to enter the dark hallway. As soon as he shut the door, she reactivated it. "Just in case. If anyone tries to let themselves in with his key, we'll know."

"Good idea," said Michael, stomping the melting snow off his boots.

"Don't worry about tracking in snow," she said. "We need to be ready to go."

He nodded. "Where is the bag?"

"It should be somewhere in the front hall closet."

"Lead the way."

The house was cold and eerily quiet. The only sounds were the swishes of their winter coats and the creak of the wooden floor under each footstep. She made her way through the kitchen, down the hallway, to the closet between the front door and the L-shaped staircase that led upstairs.

Sean's words echoed in her mind, firm and urgent over the phone line just a few hours before the terrible news of his death came in. *The bag is in the closet, under my coats.*

She had cleaned the house of most of the reminders of him, but for some reason, his clothes had been difficult. She still wasn't ready to catch a glimpse of the bare closet where his shirts and coats and boots used to be. So she had avoided this spot.

Ellie slid open the left door, Sean's side, and knelt on the floor in front of it. She peered in, ignoring the catch of her breath as she pushed aside the neat lines of boots and shoes. No bag. What was going on? Maybe she wasn't remembering correctly. Maybe he'd said, *The bag is in the closet, under your coats*? Of course, she'd been in and out of her side countless times this winter, but maybe she'd missed something. Her heartbeat ticked up as she closed one door and slid open the other, pulling out the racks from under her jackets. Still nothing. She stared at the closet.

"It's not here," she whispered.

Michael was silent.

"It has to be here. Sean mentioned it the day—" She swallowed and forced herself to finished the sentence. "The day of the accident. It was one of the last things he said to me."

The last thing he'd said was *I love you*. Those words had gotten her through the lowest of her days, when she couldn't get out of bed, and she could still hear both the urgency in his voice and the love. He *had* loved her, she told herself. She bit her lip and looked up at Michael. His jaw was set and the corners of his mouth curved downward.

"You need to go," she said. "You've already put yourself in enough danger. I can do this on my own."

"I believe you can do this on your own, Ellie," he said softly. "But I don't want to leave you alone."

His gaze was so intense. Everything in her rang with the feeling that radiated from him. *I will protect you. I will make sure you're safe.*

"But we only met a few hours ago." It was supposed to be evidence that he could let her go, but it was also a plea. *Do you want to put yourself at risk for me?*

"Yes," he said in a tone she couldn't read.

He looked down at her as a strange mixture of emotions rolled through her, strong enough to throw her off balance. The connection as she looked in his dark brown eyes was both familiar and new, both a balm and a disturbance deep inside her. She'd loved Sean, and she always would. So what was this attraction? Ellie looked away.

Michael cleared his throat. "What exactly are we looking for?"

"A small duffel bag, about this big." She gestured with her hands. "Black, rectangular, with a zipper on top."

"Any ideas about where else to look?"

There was so much churning through her mind, but she forced herself to focus. "It has to be somewhere I don't usually look, or I would have stumbled over it these last few months. I thought about it after the accident when I was in Santa Barbara, but I was in shock and sort of…forgot about it—at least until Aidan threatened me."

She could rule out the kitchen, the living room, two of the bathrooms, her bedroom…

"I'll check the extra bedrooms upstairs, and you can check the garage." She gestured to the door off the hallway. "We should split up to save time."

"I don't like the idea of splitting up," said Michael. "Both our chances are better when we're together."

His voice was soft, almost tender. And her fears echoed inside her, fears of finding herself alone again, fears that begged her to run far away from this house. But she couldn't listen to those fears. She needed a way to stop running, so she forced herself to shake her head.

"We need to get out of here as soon as possible." When he looked like he would protest, she added, "My decision."

Michael frowned. "At least let me come up with you for a quick scan of the second floor. Please?"

His hand brushed against the sleeve of her coat. His touch was too light to feel through the fabric and yet she still reacted. His touch filled her with warmth, a warmth of safety in an unsafe world, a warmth of closeness. She met his dark, expressive eyes and her cheeks heated. "Follow me."

She climbed the stairs, trying to block out the familiar feeling of regret that came with all the reminders of the life she'd lost. Everything left unsaid, unresolved. But as she turned the corner of the landing, toward the next flight to the second floor, she saw Michael come to a stop in front of an old photo of Sean and her that she'd hung in a cursory attempt to make the house feel more like a home. They were sitting on the ledge in the Grand Canyon, wearing matching

Cal State Fullerton T-shirts and hiking boots. Sean wore a baseball cap turned backward, and her hair was tied back into a ponytail that fluffed out behind her head.

"You two look happy," he said, studying the photo.

"We were…back then." *Back then.* The last two words slipped out before Ellie could stop them. Her breath caught in her throat, but the words were already out there, the betrayal hanging in the air. This wasn't the kind of thing she was supposed to say about her own marriage. Especially not after Sean's death. "I don't mean we weren't happy. It's just that things got…complicated."

Michael nodded, his gaze still fixed on the photo and its bright silver frame.

"Sharing your life with someone does get complicated." He turned to her with a hint of a smile. "At least, that's my experience."

Ellie let out a breath. Maybe it wasn't a betrayal. Maybe it was just honesty. She bit her lip and continued. "I grew up on our family's ranch up north, and Sean is from Santa Monica, but something about us matched when we met."

"Where did you meet?"

"Church service. It was the first week of my freshman year in Fullerton, and I knew no one. I was convinced I'd made a terrible mistake, traveling so far from home. But when I met Sean, everything changed. I knew I was in the right place."

Michael smiled. "Sunny and I met in college, too. San Jose State."

"Were you opposites or two of a kind?"

"Some of both. I was like you, a country boy, and she was a city girl, from San Francisco. But we had a lot in common, starting with the fact that we're both from Chinese American families. Or she…was."

He turned away.

She wanted to ask more questions, but it was clear this was hard for him to talk about. Also, they needed to get out of the house.

"Let's go," she said, and started on the flight of stairs.

Michael followed her up the steps and down the hallway as she opened each door, looking for signs of intrusion.

"Looks clear to me," she said, her hand still on the bathroom handle.

Michael's eyes met hers again and he gave her a curt nod. "Let's get this done quickly. I've got a bad feeling about being here this long."

"Me, too."

Michael headed downstairs, and she started with the guest bedroom. It was sparsely furnished, just the bed, two bedside tables carved from cedar, and a tall dresser. She searched under the bed then pulled out the dresser drawers, all empty. The closet was mostly bare, just a small stack of bed linens, another shelf of guest towels, and a set of hangers that clattered around each time she moved the door. It wasn't there.

She rushed out the door and down the hallway to the next the bedroom. That one was painted yellow, and on the closet shelves were some of the few remainders from her own childhood: a baby blanket her grandmother had knitted, a small stack of books, and three tiny dresses. The room was supposed to be for their first kid. *When things settle down*, Sean had said. Ellie pushed that thought away and pulled open more drawers and closet doors, but she still found nothing.

In the closet, under my coats.

Why would he have given her those specific details if the bag was somewhere else? It didn't make sense. A go bag wasn't the kind of thing he'd accidentally misplace.

Had someone gotten to it first? Maybe someone with access to the key had come to the house before she'd changed the alarm code… That was everyone at Green Living Construction.

It was more likely Ellie was missing something. She stood in the upstairs hallway, looking one way, then the other. Below her, she heard the creak of the garage door and the thud of Michael's boots in the downstairs hallway.

My coats…

Oh. Now she understood.

Ellie sprinted along the hallway toward the back of the house. She flung open the door to the master bedroom, ignoring the king-size bed, far too big for one person, ignoring the covered balcony just outside the sliding door with two chairs that looked out into the stretch of mountains. She didn't look at the photo on the dresser of Sean and her, taken the afternoon of their wedding on the Santa Barbara beach just after the ceremony. Instead she headed straight for the closet.

Ellie's hands trembled as she turned the knob and switched on the light to the walk-in. At the far end, past two long rows of clothes, was an enormous cedar chest, another one of the few items left from her childhood. She swept the boxes of shoes off the top and they tumbled to the floor. Ellie ignored them and lifted the lid. On the top lay an older dark blue puffy down jacket. One Sean hadn't worn in years. Her heart thumped harder. She tossed it aside and found another one below it. This one red, one he'd had since college. She pulled it out and her breath caught in her throat. Below was the duffel bag.

She'd found it.

Ellie lifted the heavy bag out of the closet and set it on the floor. Her nervous fingers fumbled with the zipper until finally she pulled it open. She stared down at the contents. On top, there were two passports, hers and Sean's, sitting on an envelope. Below these items were stacks and stacks of bills. How many were there? A hundred stacks, maybe more? She'd never seen this much money in her life. It should be enough for her to leave, to get away to somewhere far from here, all for her. A strange rush of relief ran through her. For the first time today, Ellie felt like she had a chance.

She looked at the two passports and the envelope. On the front of it, Sean had written her name in all capital letters. Her heart pounded in her chest. Oh, how she'd hoped to find something from Sean in the months since his death, some message or sign from him, but now she was afraid to open it. What if this was a door to yet another secret, something else he had kept from her?

"Not the time for this, Ellie," she whispered to herself.

They needed to get out of the house, and she needed to get Michael away from her, away from the danger she'd put him in. She shoved the letter into the pocket of her jacket, trying hard not to think about Sean's life and anything else he hadn't told her. She picked up the bag and started across the room. She had to tell Michael what she'd found and then they needed to leave—and pray that the men after them didn't catch up.

Michael opened the door and fumbled on the wall for the light. He flipped it on, and two bare fluorescent bulbs flickered to life, revealing a perfectly organized garage. No surprises there. It was much like the rest of the house: stylish and yet somehow impersonal. Sterile. The whole place reminded him of the way real estate agents decorated a home right before selling it, with furniture and art carefully chosen to portray a classy yet impersonal ambience.

It felt as if this place was still staged, long after Ellie and Sean had moved in.

Still, Michael was impressed with how organized they'd kept their house. It was the opposite of the ranch, where his family had lived for three generations. At times, the main house spilled over with guests, cousins, their kids, seasonal workers…whatever eclectic crew was around to run the ranch or just to visit. Winters were slower, but the thaw brought enough people to make this kind of order impossible. The thought of such a gathering of family and friends set off an unexpected pang of longing in his gut, longing for a time when Tang Ranch had not been inextricably connected with the loss of Sunny.

And you want to leave it all behind.

Michael pushed that thought away and stepped down onto the concrete floor. What was most striking about the strangely impersonal feel of the house was that it didn't match what he knew of Ellie, the woman who'd maneuvered her way through memory loss and danger. Not that he knew her very well, he reminded himself.

There weren't a lot of places to hide a duffel bag in the garage. On one side, mountain bikes, downhill skis and snowshoes were neatly organized with other miscellaneous outdoor equipment. The other side was bare, except for the trashcan and recycling bin. Along the back wall, two metal shelves were stacked with matching storage bins. If the duffel bag was in the garage, it had to be in one of those.

Each of the storage bins was carefully marked with labels like Ski Boots or Riding Gear. He'd have to open them all one by one. On the other side of the garage door, the wind howled. He took down the first box from the left on the top shelf, labeled Photos, keeping an ear out for other sounds from outside. Was that the hum of an engine? He listened to the drone grow closer...then pass. He pulled the lid off the bin. Peering deeper under the frames, the contents were as promised. Just piles of framed photos of Sean and Ellie.

When he'd studied the photo on the staircase, he'd focused on Sean, searching for clues about who the man was. Now he focused on Ellie's hair, tamed into a fancy twist. She was wearing a blue gown that shimmered. Her gray eyes were filled with laughter and her necklace sparkled with diamonds. Fancy, that was for sure. And confident. So different from the woman he had found running down the mountain, panicked and checking over her shoulder.

Had she gathered up all the reminders of her past life, desperate to do something about what she couldn't change? That would explain the empty, impersonal feel to the house. It had taken him at least a year to get to this point, to stop clinging to memories of his life with Sunny. That Ellie had done this so efficiently had him feeling a mix of empathy and admiration. Maybe she didn't know where to go next. Well, that made two of them.

Michael frowned and replaced the lid, then set the box back on the top shelf. He took down another then another, but no surprises lurked there. As he lifted the fifth box, the growl of an engine hummed through the garage door, this one louder than before. Michael froze, listening as it grew closer. Louder. Then the motor cut. Was the sound from a neighbor's driveway or was the vehicle on Ellie's property? Michael had a bad feeling. He shoved the bin back onto the shelf as the slam of a vehicle's door echoed over the bare concrete of the garage.

Michael raced across the garage and through the door, back into the house. The sky was darker now as he moved along the hallway and toward the front. Above him, there was silence. Should he call out to Ellie? No. The last thing he wanted was for her to rush down the stairs right now. It was best for him to scout it out first. Michael hurried into the living room, to the large picture window that looked out into the front yard. He peered from behind the curtains through the window.

There, in the middle of the driveway, was a black truck. Michael's senses switched into high alert as he searched the cab for signs of life, but the inside was dark and still. Then he saw the footprints. They started from the driver's door and looped around the vehicle, joining a set of footprints leading up to the front door. Someone was right there, at the front door.

Warn Ellie. It's not too late.

The thought raced through his mind, but before he could open his mouth to call to her, the creak of the front door echoed through the living room. Footsteps. The door snicked shut and the alarm gave a quiet chirp.

A man stood in front of him, just a few yards away, his back to Michael. He was tall, with a stocky, athletic build. His dark cap covered most of his sandy-brown hair, and he was dressed in jeans, heavy boots and a red down jacket that went to his thighs. His wide stance was confident as he jabbed at the alarm, no doubt hoping to keep it off. Was this Clint or Aidan…or someone else? Michael stood stock-still. The moment the man turned around, Michael would be exposed. That meant he couldn't get to Ellie. The intruder stood between them.

If Ellie was right, and Sean's family didn't know the code to the alarm, it would go off within the next minute. Ellie would be warned soon enough. *If she's right.* Right now, he focused on giving her the best possible chance for escape. He needed to get himself between her and danger. And Michael found that he was fully ready to do that.

He had two choices. One was to quietly cross the room and confront the man, using surprise to his advantage. The closer he got, the greater chance Michael would have the upper hand. But, at first glance, he suspected this man not only carried a gun but wouldn't hesitate to shoot first, despite the fact he was the one breaking and entering. And if he shot Michael, that would leave Ellie alone to defend herself.

No, he couldn't risk it. He'd wait for the alarm to go off and announce himself from across the room. He'd then stall while he attempted to move in, to position himself between this guy and Ellie. Michael needed to intercept the threat as soon as possible, before the man thought to head upstairs. If he could get close enough, he could take the man down—that much he was confident about. Still, the most dangerous person in any situation wasn't the strongest or the most agile. It was the person who was willing to do the most harm, the person who would throw away everything to get what he wanted. It was the person who cared more about their goal than the lives around them. This was the kind of man who would harm Michael if he stood in the way of what he wanted. And Michael was about to do exactly that.

He didn't like the idea of walking toward danger any better than the next person, and yet, as he waited for the alarm to ring, he felt the lift of a clear purpose. Ellie had suffered great loss, the same way he had, and yet she was determined to fight for her life. That idea sent a surge of energy through him, resonating deep inside. He would fight, too.

The man continued to punch away at the alarm box, punctuating each failed try with curses of frustration. Then the alarm let out a piercing wail. Another curse echoed through the living room, this one louder.

"Hello?" he called from across the room over the sound of the alarm. The man whipped around. When he caught sight of Michael, the anger in his expression shifted into surprise. He reached inside his unzipped jacket with his right hand and Michael froze. Somewhere under there was almost certainly a gun.

"Who are you and what are you doing in my brother's..." The man's voice died away, like he was recalculating the situation and wasn't liking what he was coming up with. He'd said "my brother's"—this was Aidan. His right hand lingered inside the thick, down jacket, and Michael's heart jumped in his chest. But he forced a confused look on his face and hoped Aidan would read him as nonthreatening. As they stood frozen in this dangerous tableau, Michael assessed him as an opponent. Right-handed, he noted.

The man pulled his hand out of his jacket. No gun. Instead, he stuck out his meaty hand for a handshake. "Aidan Alexander."

"Michael Tang. I'm a friend."

"A friend of Elizabeth? I'm looking for her," Aidan said, his voice grave. "She's in danger."

Michael frowned. "Danger?"

"She's my sister-in-law," the man continued in that same, serious voice. "As you might know, my brother passed away a few months ago, and since then, Elizabeth hasn't been herself. She gets herself worked up, and now she's disappeared. I'm worried about her." The words were punctuated by something Michael didn't expect—an expression of genuine concern.

As the alarm rang all around them, a tiny glimmer of doubt ran through Michael's mind. What if Aidan's explanation was true? All Michael had to go on was Ellie's account, which included amnesia.

Ellie had lost a spouse, too. That truth sat inside him, heavy, weighing him down enough that he wanted to lean against the doorjamb. She was staggering under her own loss, and he knew better than most how much that loss changed everything about a person. How it could drive a person to the edge of reason. He studied the worried look on Aidan's face. If Michael had a sister-in-law who had disappeared, he'd do everything to find her. He'd want to know where she was, that she was safe.

Still, Michael bristled at the man's comments. Something about his tone when he'd said *she gets herself worked up* made him uncomfortable, like Aidan had ideas about women that Michael didn't share. And then there were the men who had tried to kidnap Ellie—they had given the same explanation Aidan had.

He offered a neutral response. "I'm sorry for the loss of your brother."

"He's in good hands with the Lord," Aidan said. There was genuine sorrow in his expression, but it was mixed with something else Michael couldn't identify. "Elizabeth is here right now, isn't she."

It wasn't a question. Michael had to decide. He had to listen to his heart. It was pounding out a message, loud and clear: *protect Ellie.*

The alarm wailed, the piercing sound ratcheting the tension in the room even higher. Michael started across the floor, keeping an eye on Aidan's right hand. It didn't move, so Michael continued. He shoved his hands in his pockets, as if the two of them weren't in the middle of a chess game where the consequence for losing could be brutal.

"How do you know she's here?" Michael asked, stalling for time as he closed the distance between him and the man. "And how did you get in?"

A good-old-boy smile, the one that oozed both authority and charm, spread across his face.

"Sean gave me a key, but something's wrong with the alarm," said Aidan. "Elizabeth needs to turn this thing off. Where is she?"

Michael stopped in front of the staircase. He leaned against the banister, but inside readied himself for whatever was coming.

"She said she doesn't want to see you," said Michael, tilting his head to the side a little, like he was confused. "She says you tried to harm her."

Anger slashed across Aidan's face. It was gone almost instantly, but in that moment, Michael knew that he had chosen correctly. This man was hiding his fury, trying to manipulate Michael.

Aidan shook his head and grimaced. "Like I told you, she's been buried in grief, and it's making her hysterical. Paranoid. I need to bring her somewhere where she'll be safe, where she can be reasoned with. Because right now, she's not making any sense."

"What do you know about the men who came to my property, trying to take her away? Or the truck that was chasing us?" Michael asked. There was no way those men hadn't told Aidan what had happened, so Michael put it out in the open, drawing out the conversation.

Aidan assessed him. "The foreman at our construction company is a buddy of mine, and he and another guy are helping me find Elizabeth." He shook his head. "But they got a bit heavy-handed. Not my intention. I just want her to be safe."

It was a plausible explanation...if Michael hadn't actually been there. But he could see the way Aidan's carefully crafted explanation sketched a story of a reasonable, worried brother-in-law just trying to take care of his unstable sister-in-law. He was painting a picture, not just for Michael, but for everyone they might encounter.

Michael didn't believe the way Aidan was shaping the story. He believed what Ellie had insisted—that she was in danger. But he was impressed with just how convincing Aidan's account was. And that made him uneasy. Ellie's hesitation to contact the police was making more and more sense. He could see why a friend on the police force might believe the man's story. That made Aidan even more dangerous. Here was a man who was willing to use his power to manipulate others, to take away Ellie's power, her choices. And that was something that Michael would never stand for.

The alarm was wearing on Michael, that incessant, high-pitched wail. Somewhere, a company was being signaled, alerted by the intruder, but up here at the top of the Sierra Nevada, in the middle of a winter storm, alarms were a joke. The best anyone could hope for was a visit from the company after the roads were cleared. Long after this would be over. Aidan undoubtedly knew this was true.

"Where is she?" Aidan repeated, taking a step closer. "She needs to come down and turn off the alarm."

He took another step. The man was trying to intimidate Michael. Good. The nearer he was, the better.

"I imagine she doesn't trust being close to you, considering the events of the day," said Michael mildly.

Aidan advanced another step and Michael straightened. He took his hands out of his pockets, preparing himself for whatever came next. The alarm squealed over and over. Michael could see the tension in the man's jaw, the way the noise was wearing on him, too.

"I'm going upstairs to find her," said Aidan, his voice taking on an edge, losing some of that jovial good-old-boy tone. "She needs to come down and take care of this."

Michael shook his head. "I can't let you do that."

Aidan's expression hardened and Michael caught a flash of anger, unfiltered. He had seen glimpses of it simmering under the surface, but Aidan was no longer holding back. Michael could see exactly why Ellie would run from him.

"What makes you think I need your permission?" the man said through gritted teeth. "I need Elizabeth, and this isn't your house."

Aidan took another step, so that he was within arm's reach. Good. No one with any real plan would let themselves get that close. This was a man who hadn't thought further than intimidation. But the wild card was the gun. Michael knew this kind of man would have one. It was just a question of where and how hard it would be to disarm him.

Aidan took one more step to the side, like he was going to go around Michael and up the stairs. He tried to nudge Michael aside, but Michael grabbed Aidan's right arm and twisted it behind his back. Aidan let out a yelp of surprise and flailed his free arm, trying to grab hold of Michael. He yanked Aidan's right arm higher, forcing the man to double over.

Aidan kicked back at Michael, throwing them both off balance. Together, they tipped sideways, falling on the wooden steps. Michael tried to twist before they hit, but his shoulder crashed into the edge of the wooden plank. Pain shot down his biceps and he fought to keep hold of the man's arm. The grunt from under him told Michael that the fall hadn't been good for Aidan either. More of the man's curses came through under the screech of the alarm.

"I should have guessed you knew karate," he muttered.

Michael ignored the barb—maybe intentional or maybe ignorance? He almost laughed. Did this guy even know what karate was? "These are high school wrestling moves, buddy. Mixed with some self-defense."

Aidan struggled under Michael's hold, his left arm grasping inside his jacket.

The gun. Aidan was going for it.

Michael had to reach it first.

But Aidan's right side was crushed against the staircase. Michael found footing against the wall behind him and kicked hard. He and Aidan rolled so that Michael was now on top of the other man. Michael reached around to the inside of his jacket, but before he got there, Aidan pulled out the gun with his left hand. His nondominant hand. This was possibly even more dangerous.

"Michael. He has a gun." Ellie's voice broke through the pitch of the alarm, and both Michael and Aidan shifted toward it.

"Get behind the wall," Michael shouted.

As the last word came out of his mouth, the gun went off, a thundering boom over the wail of the alarm. Fear surged through Michael's body, a cold echo inside him. Had Ellie been hit? *Not her, Lord. Please, not again.* Michael couldn't see her. He had to make sure she was all right. That meant he had to disarm this man now. He tugged hard against Aidan's arm, tightening his hold, distracting him as he reached for the left arm. When he caught it, he banged it against the edge of the stairs, once, twice, harder each time.

"You should be protecting her, not threatening her," Michael muttered.

Aidan's grip began to loosen, so Michael rapped the man's knuckles again and again until, finally, the gun clattered onto the step. The moment Aidan let go, Michael twisted his left arm behind him. Now both arms were secure. Aidan struggled underneath him, but the man was stuck. The problem was, so was Michael. The moment he moved, Aidan would be up, too. But Michael could deal with that once Ellie was safe.

Please, don't let her be hurt.

"Ellie? Are you all right up there?"

A pause. One second stretched out into another, infinite, as he teetered on the edge of panic. "Ellie?"

"Yes." Her voice was soft, barely audible over the alarm.

Thank you, Lord.

"I need you to come down here," he called. "Get his gun. I have a hold on him so he can't get up."

Aidan renewed his struggles, kicking and bucking as Michael tried to take a glimpse up the stairs. Finally, Ellie's red curls peeked out from behind the wall, then her face. She looked at them, like she was assessing the situation for herself. Slowly, she started down.

When she was a few steps away, Aidan whispered something Michael didn't catch. Ellie swayed, gripping the banister, as a look of devastation crossed her face. *Stay strong*, he silently pleaded. Then she straightened, let go of the banister, and continued down the stairs.

Aidan barked, "You both are going to regret this."

"That's funny," she said. "I'd think you were the one with the regrets at this moment."

Aidan growled. As she took the last steps, he lurched toward her, but Michael pulled hard on his right arm.

"Steady," muttered Michael, who then turned to Ellie. "Pick up the gun."

Ellie scowled down at it and then picked it up, keeping it pointed at the floor.

"Now go out the back door," he said over the alarm. "Take your snowmobile and get away from here."

Ellie stared at him with that hard look of determination. "There's no way I'm leaving you behind."

SEVEN

Fear jolted through Ellie like a live wire to her system. *Aidan's voice.* A dark cloud of dread came over her.

Her breaths came faster as she neared a full-system panic. The attack outside the cave came back in full detail: the way he had yelled at her, overpowered her, the stars that had crept into her vision as the world faded away.

Now it was happening again. Ellie took a deep breath. Another. Was she having some sort of breakdown? Aidan's comment back in the cave came back. *This is your fault, Elizabeth*, he'd hissed. *All of it.*

How could she be sure that she could trust anything else about herself right now? The echoes of her past were determined to swamp her.

She'd thought they could come and go from the house without being caught, but as she'd crossed the hallway, go bag in hand, the alarm pierced through the house. For a moment, she'd considered bringing it with her, but what if the intruder got ahold of the only money? So she'd shoved a few things into her jacket and thrown the go bag into the cabinet below the bathroom sink. Then she'd waited, listening as Aidan had spun a new version of events for Michael.

What if Michael believed Aidan over her? She knew she'd been acting odd, secretive, and she wasn't even sure she could trust herself. Michael might give her away, either accidentally or intentionally. Ellie closed her eyes and prayed. She prayed for help, and she prayed for calm, for a way out of this panic. *Trust God. He will guide you. Trust God. It's the only thing you have right now.*

But... *This is your fault, Elizabeth. All of it.*

Ellie had almost tripped down the steps as those words rattled through her, warring with the calm she was desperately grasping for. The fragment of that morning in the cave had come back, just a flash of words and emotions. *Your fault.* Those words, the cold that had seeped through her wet boots, all the way up to her neck, and the sinking pit of dread inside, the dread of being trapped by him. *Your fault.*

Ellie's heart jumped in her chest. She had to keep it together, for her sake but also for Michael's.

Anger shone from Aidan's eyes as he looked up at her, struggling under Michael's firm hold.

The alarm wailed, over and over, incessant, demanding her attention. She ignored it, ignored that fragment of memory. She had to close all her memories off and focus on the gun. Get it far away from Aidan.

She swallowed, feeling the weight of it in her hand. She hated guns, hated the one Sean had kept in the house, even after she told him about the time her neighbor had accidentally shot her father in the arm. It had left her dad with chronic pain, a pile of medical bills, and a ranch that her parents could no longer keep up with on their own.

But I'm careful, Sean had said. *We should have one, just in case.*

In what case would he have shot someone? She hadn't pushed the point with him and, truthfully, she was glad she'd never know. It was the first thing she had gotten rid of after he'd died. And now there was another one in the house.

"Ellie, go!" Michael shouted.

She looked down at him.

But, like she'd told him, there was no way on earth she was leaving him behind.

Instead, she shook her head, took out the bullet cartridge and walked into the kitchen, out of Aidan's line of sight. She stopped in the middle of the room, looking across the sleek counters, scanning the modern white cabinets. Where could she put the gun? She couldn't keep it with her—just holding it made her hand shake. The trash was out of the question. Somewhere where Aidan would never look. She could get rid of it later... She opened the pantry door, scanned the shelves, and shoved it behind a roll of paper towels. She closed the door quietly, as the alarm continued to squeal. At least the noise blocked out the sound of her movements.

Ellie studied the room again, the cartridge like a live hand grenade in her palm. The silverware drawer? No. Maybe inside one of the mixing bowls? Better. She opened the cabinet door and deposited the heavy black case between two stacks of stainless-steel bowls, then ran back down the hallway.

Michael strained to keep Aidan under control. How much longer would he last? She crossed into the front entryway and tapped in the code to disarm the alarm. The sound died, leaving her ears ringing in the silence.

"You're going to pay for this," Aidan hissed into the silence, shifting under Michael's grip to look at her. She avoided his glare, focusing on Michael.

"What do you need?" she asked him.

He hesitated. "A rope?"

Had she come across one in the frenzy of cleaning she'd done after Sean had died? Nothing that she could remember.

"I don't think we have anything thicker than kitchen twine."

"What about duct tape?"

"I'll find something. Be right back," she said, and headed for the garage.

"You know you'll pay for this," said Aidan as she stepped past him. "I will never forget this. It will haunt you for the rest of your life."

Ellie was trying to ignore him, trying to ignore the shudder that ran through her body, but she knew he was serious. He'd warned her before: he would never leave her alone.

Worry about that later. One problem at a time.

She opened the door and headed for the tool bench. She opened the toolbox, pulling out wrenches and pliers. No duct tape. Ellie raced across the garage to the stack of moving boxes, scanning the labels for something useful. Clothes, photos…her sewing basket? Opening the box, she moved aside her blue fabric scissors and a handful of spools of thread but stopped at a coil of red grosgrain ribbon. That might work. She grabbed the coil and the scissors and ran back into the house.

Michael grunted under the weight of Aidan's kicks. Aidan had started a full-on assault of Michael, swearing at him, calling him every terrible thing he could imagine. Michael's expression was focused as he maneuvered to stay on top of the other man. If Aidan's words were getting to Michael, he wasn't letting on.

"Start with his knees," said Michael. "Tie them together."

Aidan kicked and swore as Ellie wound the ribbon around his legs, dodging his feet. She pulled his knees together and tied it, cutting off some of the flailing, then cut the coil free.

"I need Elizabeth alive, at least for now, but I don't need you," said Aidan through gritted teeth.

What did that mean?

"Good job," said Michael, ignoring Aidan's curses. "Now, his ankles."

That proved harder, she thought as a wet boot grazed her face, just missing her nose. Also, the knot that tied his knees was already loosening. He'd moved around enough that the knot wasn't as tight as she'd thought. But how long could Michael hold him there? This was the best she could do.

She managed to get his ankles together and pulled the knot as hard as she could, wishing she hadn't dropped out of 4-H at such a young age. Maybe then her knots would hold better.

"You're doing great, Ellie," said Michael as Aidan muttered more threats. "Now drop the ribbon and the scissors next to me."

She lay them on the stairs.

"You don't have time to clean off your own snowmobile. We need to take mine," he said. "The key is in the left pocket of my coat."

Ellie's breath caught in the back of her throat. "I told you I wouldn't leave you."

Michael winced as Aidan's elbow hit his side. "I'll be right behind you."

Ellie met his stare, his brown eyes steady and serious.

"Trust me," he whispered.

Those words echoed inside her, trying to take hold. She had trusted Sean, and this was where it'd gotten her. But what was the alternative?

Ellie swallowed a quick breath and nodded. She reached for his pocket and fumbled for the key inside. After one more glance at Aidan and Michael, she turned away and ran down the hallway. The helmets sat on the kitchen counter. She grabbed them both and flew out the back door.

The cold was a jolt to her system as she trampled through the snow, heading down the deck stairs to the snowmobile. The machine was covered in a new layer of powder. Ellie quickly brushed it off and sat down, fit the key into the ignition, and turned it. The snowmobile shuddered once and died.

No. Please no.

She tried again. The motor sputtered and then raced to life. She turned the vehicle to point out, facing the open mountain. And waited. Waited.

Please, God, don't let Michael come to harm. Not this man.

Ellie tried to settle her mind, to focus on their best escape route, but as she stared at the door, worry clattered around in her brain. What if Aidan came out first? How long did she wait until she went back in to help? The memory that Aidan had loosened rattled around with the rest of her thoughts. What was her fault? Whatever it was, it had shaken her.

The door burst open and Michael ran out, his coat flying wide behind him as he bounded through the powder and scrambled onto the snowmobile.

Ellie's heart jumped as Aidan flew out of the house after him, coming straight for them.

"Hold on," she said.

Michael grabbed his helmet, leaned against her, and wrapped his arms around her. "I'm on. *Go.*"

Ellie gunned the motor, launching them into the endless white landscape.

"Head left, toward my property," Michael said through the intercom.

He knew every inch of the land, even covered in layers

of snow. That gave them an advantage—one they sorely needed.

Because that was too close. Much too close. Ellie turned the snowmobile. They raced away from the house. As they neared the clump of trees that lined the back of her property, a gunshot rang out from behind them over the mountainside. Another. And another.

Ellie gunned the motor again and they wove behind the trees and down the mountain.

"You okay?" she asked.

"He missed me," he said, panting. "You?"

"Fine."

"I wouldn't call this fine," he said dryly. "What happened with the gun?"

"I hid it in the pantry, and the bullets were across the room. There's no way he had time to find them when he was chasing you out."

Michael frowned. "Now we know that Aidan has another gun."

She had tied Aidan's feet as best she could with the ribbon, but Michael had known it wouldn't last long. And without someone to hold Aidan down, he wasn't able to do much better with the man's hands. But there was no way he'd keep Ellie in the house while he let go of Aidan. Both their odds were better when he wasn't worried about her safety. Something had crossed her face while Aidan had spouted his threats at her, something Michael couldn't quite read. She had looked…shaken.

Getting out of the house ahead of Aidan hadn't been easy. Michael had held the man's arms behind his back until he could hear the whir of the snowmobile motor. Until he was sure that Ellie could get to safety. He had managed to shift both Aidan's wrists into one hand while he'd grabbed the ribbon, but tying a knot one-handed was hopeless. And, sure enough, as soon as Michael had moved, Aidan was already loosening the knots. Michael had bought them those precious few moments, enough to grab the scissors and get him out of the house, so he'd taken those minutes and run. And he'd made it. They'd gotten away. For now.

Thank you, Lord.

"A little further to the left," he said, straining to see through the darkening landscape. "Up there, just past those trees."

"I see them."

"Watch your speed here. The boulders are hard to see when it starts to get dark." If they drove over the back of one of the big ones and crashed the snowmobile in the fall, they'd have a whole new set of problems.

Ellie slowed the machine as they entered the forest that marked the boundary to Tang Ranch land. It was home, where Michael knew exactly how to navigate. *Home.* He hadn't felt this surge of comfort from the ranch in a long time. He pushed that thought away and focused on the landscape.

"We need a plan," he said as she wove through the trees. "We need to find a place to stop."

He pointed to a large boulder sticking up into the trees and covered in white. "Right there. On top."

The height would give them a good view of their surroundings. The falling darkness had one advantage: they could see the lights of any vehicle from much farther away. Ellie slowed to a stop on top of the large mound, then turned off the motor. The headlight flickered off. Michael could hear Ellie's rapid breaths through the intercom.

"That was a mistake to go back," she said quietly.

"You needed to try." He did understand that part.

Michael climbed off the snowmobile and sunk into the deep snow. He pulled off his helmet and stretched his arms. His right biceps was throbbing from the fall on the steps, and Aidan had gotten a couple good jabs into his ribs that still ached. And she hadn't even found what she'd come for. Or had she?

"Any sign of the go bag?"

Ellie took off her helmet and her bright curls sprang out from underneath, like they'd been waiting to escape.

"I found it right about when the alarm went off. I…" She blew out a breath. "I was scared Aidan would get a hold of it, so I left the bag in the closet."

"You're not going back in there." The words came out more forcefully than he had intended. Michael laced his fingers behind his head and looked up at the sky. They weren't going to get anywhere if he talked to her like that. "Please. Tell me you're not planning to go back."

She shook her head slowly. "At least not now. I grabbed a few things. It's not much, but…" Her voice trailed off. She tugged off her gloves and dropped them in her lap, then unzipped the black ski shell he'd lent her. From the inside pocket, she pulled out a stack of twenty-dollar bills, two passports and an envelope.

"I didn't get a chance to look at this," she said, holding up the envelope. "A letter from Sean. I can't tell you how much I wanted to find some sort of message from him those first few months after he was gone. Now… I'm not so sure."

He just nodded, trying not to pry. The clouds had scattered and patches of sky were lit with distant sunset somewhere behind the mountains, turning the tops of the gray clouds shades of purple. Motors buzzed in the background, but he couldn't see anything on their side of the mountain.

"How dangerous would it be to rest right now?" she asked, rubbing the back of her head.

Michael came on full alert. "Is your head hurting you?"

"Just a little."

"We can rest," he said quickly.

The adrenaline was still pumping through his veins, telling him to run, to get away from there, but he knew better than to listen to that. She had been running on empty all morning. If they didn't rest soon, she was going to crash. Michael looked around at the opening through the trees, down the vast mountainside. It was cold but clear, at least, for the moment. If they were going to stop, now was probably the safest time. When they had shaken Aidan—at least for now. But first, he needed to get her somewhere safe.

"It's getting dark," said Michael. "We need shelter."

"But we can't lead Aidan back to your ranch."

"Agreed." He pictured his parents, his grandparents, Isabel and the new hires gathering in the main house for supper. How much would Isabel tell them about his conversation with her? "There's a fire tower on the other side of our property, above the canyon. No one uses it during the winter."

"How far?"

"Maybe a mile," he said. "Can you make it?"

"I'll make sure I do. But you should drive."

EIGHT

Ellie held on tight to Michael as they drove through the snow along the dusky landscape. The blanket of white spread over the forest floor, with pine trees and granite boulders jutting out of the earth. It would be too easy to get lost out here.

"The fire lookout is up along this next ridge," said Michael, his voice in her ear, rising above the buzz of the motor. "A buddy of mine is a park ranger, and I've helped him do some clearing over the years around here. He won't mind us stopping in to use it, as long as it's empty."

Ellie gave a little shiver at the idea of seeing anyone else. Though most of her memories were back, that fear lingered, hovering over those last ones that were still buried. She couldn't shake the feeling Aidan's words had set off inside her. *Your fault.* Was she responsible for Sean's death? That was impossible—he'd died in a car accident—and yet his brother's accusation resonated. Aidan must have revealed something to her in that cave, something her mind still did not want to go back to.

Right now, she needed to be somewhere she felt safe. Especially since the envelope was burning a hole in her pocket, the one with Sean's handwriting scrawled across the front. With Michael on the mountain, before they had entered her house, she had told him she was ready to be on her own, and she'd meant it. Now that she understood who and where she was, she didn't *need* his help anymore, strictly speaking. But as the relief had rushed through her when Michael had refused to leave, she'd realized how much she wanted him to stay, and not just for the kind of protection he had given her back at the house. Something within her felt settled when she was near him.

The snowmobile raced up the incline toward the ridge. As she gazed out across the dark valley, she saw it: a white tower poking out over the trees.

"I don't see any lights inside," said Michael. "That's a good sign it's empty."

Thank you, Lord. She needed a little time to regroup, even if the peace was temporary.

They crossed the ridge, weaving around pines until they came to a stop next to the tower. The building was probably three stories high and shaped much like a lighthouse. The lower parts were mostly wood, painted white, but the top floor was lined with windows. Perfect for looking out—or for seeing inside, if anyone approached. To reach the lookout, an outside staircase wove back and forth up to a deck that surrounded the top floor.

"I'm driving the snowmobile around the building, just to be sure we're alone," said Michael.

The darkness was a good sign, but they needed more than that.

"I don't see any tracks—at least, not human ones," she commented, studying the ground as they moved.

There were tracks—deer as well as something bigger. She shivered, not wanting to guess what else was lurking out in the darkness.

"That's the first piece of good news we've had in a while,"

said Michael wryly as he stopped the sled at the bottom of the staircase.

She took off her helmet and climbed off. Michael grabbed the backpack from the compartment under the seat.

Much of the first flight of the staircase was buried in the snow, but the wind had brushed most of it off the remainder of the steps. She followed Michael as they climbed up to the quiet, dark tower. He stopped in front of the wood door and lifted the metal flap of the lockbox.

"We can stop here for a while and come up with a plan, but we can't spend the night," he said, punching in a code. A box with a key came out, and Ellie breathed a sigh of relief. "There aren't any blankets, and any fire will tip him off to where we are. I'm not sure we want to risk that. But it's a chance to regroup and refuel."

Michael unlocked the door and entered the tiny place. Ellie followed, stomping snow off her boots. It was a room, no bigger than her bedroom back at the house. The furniture ran along the walls, under the tall windows that lined the space. Everything in the place looked like it was from the last century. There were two single beds and a small kitchen counter with a sink and cabinets. Along one wall was an old-fashioned propane stove, the only heat source, as far as she could tell, and in the corner next to it, there was a wooden table, covered with a blue-and-white-checked vinyl tablecloth and two chairs. In the center of the room was a stand made out of wood just as old as everything else, and on that stand was some sort of brass contraption. It looked a little like a sundial, but with movable parts. She moved to take a closer look.

"It's for measuring the exact location of fires. You line up the pin and the needle with the fire, and the compass points give you the location."

He came up next to her and pointed to the markings around the rotating disk.

"It's lovely," she said. "The whole place is."

"It is." There was a wispy hint of nostalgia in his voice. "Let's sit down."

Ellie collapsed onto one of the kitchen chairs and glanced out the window. A bank of clouds rolled over the dark valley. "Sean and I never really spent time in the area, and definitely not out in the wilderness. The house was supposed to be temporary, and I guess we never got around to thinking about it in any other way." She gestured to the landscape. "The strange thing is, I prefer this little lookout to the house."

"Your house was a little warmer," he said, rubbing his gloved hands together.

She looked at the view of the mountains in every direction. Above them, rocky peaks jutted up into the clouds, and all around, pine forests spread out under the blanket of snow. Ellie set her helmet on the floor next to Michael's, and he unzipped the backpack and pulled out a thermos. Ellie's mouth watered as he unscrewed the lid and poured hot chocolate into the cup. He offered her the tiny metal cup, and she took a long drink. The sweet, warm liquid danced inside her, giving her a burst of energy.

"Your friend must love being a ranger up here."

"He does, but this place hasn't been used as a fire tower since the 1930s," said Michael. "It's a camping rental, but the forest service keeps it up."

"It's so quiet," she said. "I'd love to come back here some other time."

"Sunny and I always meant to ride the horses up here and stay a night." He shook his head. "That wasn't our path."

"Sounds like the path was rough for both of you."

Ellie's mind raced as she thought about all the questions she had for him. She didn't want to pry, but as she looked across the table at this man, she felt a connection. And connections only grew if both people were willing to share parts of themselves.

Was that a step he wanted to take?

She wanted to try. "How did you meet?"

"In a study group for calculus. Neither of us were very good at it," he said with a wry smile. "Luckily, the class came more easily for our other partner, Jimena. I knew I wanted to ask Sunny out right away, but I waited until after finals. If she turned me down, neither of us could give up the study group, which would have been painfully awkward. But it turned out she was thinking the same thing."

Ellie gave him a small smile. "You met your perfect match in college, but it turned out not to be forever. Sounds familiar."

Michael laughed, those lines in the corners of his eyes creasing. It was so brief, but in that moment she could see another side of him, one filled with joy and laughter, not sorrow.

"I think my biggest regret is getting caught up in arguments and irritations in that time after the diagnosis," he said, and the last of the laughter died in his voice. "Why did I use our time together like that?"

A surge of empathy and closeness rushed through Ellie. The closeness that came from a deeper understanding, not just of him but of herself. She'd never talked about it, but she felt the same way.

"I've thought about that a lot, too," she said. "In the year leading up to Sean's death, he was so distant, so secretive. He took what he called 'business trips,' but he didn't say where. And I knew something was going on with his company, but he was vague, and I didn't push him. What if I had probed a little more? I trusted that he'd come to me when he was ready, but it never happened."

Michael looked out the window. "I had a long time to prepare, but still I held back so much. All the things I didn't ask her because I was afraid it would hurt, all the conversations she tried to have with me but I stopped. I was just so scared of losing her." He shook his head then looked at her. "I can't imagine the shock of what you went through, but I guess what I'm saying is that losing someone slowly is terribly painful, too."

Ellie swallowed, determined not to turn away from the pain he was exposing to her. "How long were you together?"

"Almost ten years."

Almost. It was like being trapped on the wrong side of a chasm, impossible to cross, and seeing the life you missed on the other side.

"I try to remember to be thankful now, even in difficult times…" She smiled. "Like today, for example. Thank you for helping me. Without you, I don't know where I'd be right now."

Michael nodded, studying her for a moment, and then a little smile cracked on his face. "I definitely wouldn't be here right now without you."

Ellie laughed. "I'm pretty sure you're getting the short end of the stick on this one."

She offered the cup of hot chocolate to Michael. He took a drink. "I'm not so sure about that."

Something about the softness of his voice made her heart quicken.

Michael stuck his hand in his backpack and pulled out homemade granola bars, a package of almonds and two oranges. He spread them out over the tablecloth.

"We both need to eat," he said. "We have no idea what the night will bring."

The comment made her shiver in fear. Would Aidan or his workers trace their path here? Even without them, there were plenty of dangers on the mountain.

Ellie took another warm drink and grabbed a handful of almonds. Then she took a deep breath and reached into her jacket pocket for the envelope. She still wasn't sure if she was ready, but she couldn't put it off any longer.

She opened the sealed flap. As she pulled out the folded paper inside, a shiny brass key slid out with it, tumbling onto the table. Michael picked it up, studied it, then placed it in the palm of her hand. Her skin was bright pink and trembling—from the cold or something more? Maybe it was both. She stared at the key for a moment then slid it back in the envelope. Her gaze settled on the folded letter. She opened it, her heart pounding.

Dear Elizabeth,
If you are reading this, it's because I need you to go ahead of me. Leave my passport in the chest for me, and leave some of the money. I promise I will be right behind you. Follow the directions to the safe house I've found for us and wait for me. The place is ours, and no one knows about it. Trust me. And tell no one you're leaving. No one.
All my love, Sean

The letter was typed, but the words *No one* were double underlined with blue ink. Below the letter was a map of the Virgin Islands and instructions for which planes to take, which buses, how many times to switch taxis to make sure no one was following her. Sean had thought through this very carefully. That meant he had understood the danger he could be in—danger he'd been exposing them both to.

Ellie felt an unexpected surge of anger at her husband, who, despite his love for her, had put them both in danger. He had loved her, hadn't he?

"What does it say?"

She swallowed visibly. "It's...it's instructions for a place. In the Virgin Islands?"

She handed Michael the letter and looked at him expectantly, like she needed confirmation that it was real. He took the letter and read it. She didn't feel the tears spilling over until Michael looked up at her. She brushed them away and gave a wry little laugh. "Some good that promise to 'be right behind me' was."

Michael reached across the table as if to take her hand, but instead he looked away.

"When I was searching through your garage, I saw pictures of you and Sean," he said.

"I took them all down after he died. I just couldn't walk around the house seeing a picture of this life of ours that was gone."

"I understand," he said. "From everything I could see in those photos, you looked happy together."

"I thought we were." But how could that be true when Sean had been hiding something this important from her? She shook her head. "I don't know what to believe anymore."

Ellie's eyes moved down to the letter again as color flooded her cheeks. Her brow knitted and her lips moved, but no words came out. Michael thought back to the photo he'd found of her with Sean in the Grand Canyon. She'd had the kind of smile full of love that reminded him of the way he used to feel. Would either of them smile like that again?

He hadn't talked much about Sunny to anyone, but maybe she would get some comfort from it. Maybe he would, too.

"Sunny and I had this dream to turn an old cabin into a little retreat for us—the line camp where I found you on our property. It's nothing much, but it was supposed to be a place for just the two of us." He shook his head slowly. "That's not what God intended for us.

"I've tried to live with all these reminders of the life we wanted together. But it's hurting my parents to see me suffer, and my pain isn't going away." He glanced at Ellie for signs of judgment, but there were none. "I'm leaving this summer. I've tried to make sure the ranch can run without me. I told them it was just for a few months, to get myself back on my feet. But if God wanted me to stay…"

Had Ellie, too, doubted God's path?

"How did your parents take that news?" she asked.

"Not well." They'd started a full-scale campaign of guilt.

"I can't do anything, even pretend to understand what God has in store for me," she said. "But I know, when Sean died, there were moments I was so angry. Angry at him for dying. Angry at myself for keeping my thoughts to myself to make our marriage run more smoothly. Angry at God for allowing this loss." She let out a long sigh. "One of my good friends from childhood stayed with me those first weeks. She reminded me of my sixteen-year-old self, worried about our ranch, with no idea where my life would take me. I never could have pictured where I would be now. So, I decided I would just trust that I have no idea what's in store. I can't imagine it. All I can do is trust it."

Michael met her gaze as the weight of her words sank

in. All she could do is trust it. God had given him a loving and close family, and a good life on the ranch. God had led him to Sunny, a woman he'd loved with all his heart. He had accepted all of this as God's will when it had brought him happiness, but now, when he had felt the pain of life, he was no longer ready to accept it? Whose life was only full of the good moments?

He looked over at Ellie, thinking about her words, her wisdom as she navigated roads not so different from his.

"I wish it felt like the good outweighed the sadness," he said.

She gave him a hint of a smile. "Don't we all. But that's not always how life works."

"I guess not," he said softly.

That feeling that had been growing inside him all day... At first, he'd dismissed it as some combination of attraction and loneliness, but this was something else. A connection. It was so different than the connection he'd had with Sunny, and yet it felt strong. Maybe it was the desperation of the situation. Or maybe he wasn't ready to think about what else it could mean.

Michael braced himself for the hurt that always came with the words he was about to speak. "Sunny, my wife, died a couple years ago. Uterine cancer." Why was it so hard to say this, even after two years of living without her? "She was funny. Kind. She saw the best in people, even the ones that disappointed her."

Ellie turned, and her gray eyes were full of emotion. "I'm so sorry. She sounds wonderful."

He nodded. "After two years trying to get pregnant, I wanted her to go to the doctor. I said it was for fertility, but the truth was, I was worried. She worked at a start-up, with late long hours. It was the kind that gave employees unlimited vacation time but pressured them never to take any of it. She was getting thinner, working long days in a tech job. I thought it was the stress." He steeled himself against the memory of what had come next. It never got easier. "She refused. She said God would give us a baby when it was time. And so I never spoke up, never told her my worries. After she fainted in the bathroom at the office the first time, I should have pushed harder. I'll always regret that. The second time, someone called an ambulance, and the hospital's tests told us it was too late. Stage 4."

He took a long breath, and looked back up at her. Ellie's eyes were wide and serious, but he didn't find pity there. Just understanding.

He exhaled slowly. "I know I can't turn back time. And if it was God's will that she was to die, I have to accept that. I just wish we had used our time better."

Ellie nodded. "I know exactly what you mean."

"I'll always regret not telling her how worried I was, how much I wanted her to get more tests," he said, looking off into the snowy landscape. They were in their own little world, secluded, safe here together in an unsafe world. "So many times I've asked myself why I didn't. I guess I didn't want to scare her, to hurt her. I was afraid the distance between us would grow. More than it already had." He looked at her. "But it had nothing to do with a lack of love."

Michael took off his glove and swiped a hand over his face. "I guess what I'm trying to say is maybe Sean had reasons that made sense at the time. Maybe he even thought he was doing what was best for you."

"Thanks for telling me," she said softly. "There are so many questions I have about that accident. We were supposed to go on vacation, but we stayed home because I canceled our weekend away. What if I had insisted, put my foot down? You don't want to do that in a marriage, to make things into conflicts, but what if I had? A little conflict would've been better than this."

Michael could feel the weight of her words as she spoke.

"I'm never going to get over Sean," Ellie added quietly.

"And I don't think I can ever say goodbye to Sunny, but it does feel good to have someone to talk to." At least for now.

She gave him a little smile and started to speak, but a flash of light through the trees cut off her words. Michael whipped around and saw a single beam pointing in their direction.

"A snowmobile," she whispered. "I wonder if it's Aidan. He could have found the spare key to mine and followed our tracks."

Michael frowned. "We can't take the chance."

"He said he needed me alive for now. What does he need from me?"

"If you died…" He swallowed, trying to keep his voice even. "Who would inherit your share of the business?"

"My parents." Ellie's brow wrinkled. "Does this put them in danger, too?"

She shoved the envelope back into the inside pocket of her jacket, and Michael began to stuff the food into the backpack. They stood.

"Are you willing to go to the police?" he asked.

"Not now. Not unless I have some sort of proof that he's lying about me," she said. "There's evidence of his bribes, but nothing that makes him look threatening. The danger to me is still his word against mine. Maybe there's something I can dig up in the files, something more solid, but it will take time. Right now, I need to get away from him."

"What about the ski resort on the other side of the mountain? They have a hotel and enough people there that we could lose him in the crowd." Michael weighed the option. "Aman, a high school friend of mine, manages the hotel portion of the resort. Sunny and I have been there a handful of times to ski with him and his wife."

But, like all his other friends, Michael had barely spoken to Aman since Sunny's funeral. He didn't even know if his friend still worked here. Once again, she would have to put her life in his hands, and it made him even more determined to live up to that trust.

The snowmobile light was getting closer.

"Let's do it."

NINE

The motor sawed underneath them as they made their way over the rugged terrain. Each time Ellie glanced behind her, she caught flashes of light through the forest. Their own headlight dipped and leaped as Michael steered across each mound, making it impossible to get a good view of the darkening landscape in front of them. Ellie was glad he was doing the driving now, though she didn't like the way it gave her brain time to hop between fear and revelation. The calm from the fire lookout was gone as Ellie forced herself to concentrate on the present. Michael navigated the snowmobile through the trees, avoiding the steep drops that seemed to come without warning. Thank God, he was handling the terrain. She would have certainly tipped the sled at some point—or worse.

The new storm was still heading for them. Above, patches of dark blue evening sky shone through the gray clouds. A clear sky would be good for visibility—for them, but also for Aidan. As it was, Aidan was getting closer, and if they slowed down, it was just a question of when he'd catch up with them.

Ellie's arms were wrapped tightly around Michael's jacket and she felt a warm comfort as she leaned against his broad back. It was the same warmth she had felt as he'd burst out of the house, unharmed, and when she'd watched his strength and agility as he'd subdued Aidan. Yes, that was what she felt right now. Comfort. And gratitude. Not attraction, or anything that conflicted with her love for Sean. Sean, whom she had trusted without question. Who had kept secrets from her. Secrets that had left her running for her life.

Ellie looked over Michael's shoulder in the direction they were headed. Mountains rose above them, steep and full of snow that the last of the sunset painted a deep, hazy purple. How long until they reached the ski resort from here? It was miles away.

"We can stay off the road a little longer," said Michael through the intercom. "But we're coming close to the slide. We'll have to take the road for that stretch."

Angel's Slide was a half mile of sharp curves that wound around the edge of the steepest part of the mountain. Ellie had heard that, before the development was built, the road used to close during winters because of the heavy snows. But now, closing the road meant cutting off the new houses to basic services, like firetrucks and ambulances, from the nearest town. In the other direction, the national forest stretched on for miles before reaching civilization again. Aidan and Sean had gone to city planning meeting after meeting, arguing to get the road maintained during the winter—and losing. And then the committee reversed its findings. Now that Ellie was part owner and had read through the documents, she understood the win was despite geologists' protests. And it had come right after a flurry of emails with two committee members about campaign donations and "gift" trips to Hawaii. But she needed to get all the evidence together and figure out who to give it to—someone not under the influence of Aidan and Clint.

Two winters ago, the plowing had triggered an avalanche that had left the road covered in dirt and gravel long, long after the snow had melted, cutting off the development from the town well into the summer. It was one of the reasons that Green Living Construction had had a hard time selling off the parcels of land. That was how Ellie had ended up with a house there. Now, as Michael steered them toward Angel's Slide, she wondered what would have happened if she'd pressed Sean with more of her questions and worries. What if she'd spoken up? Would Sean still be alive?

Ellie pushed that thought away and focused on the path ahead. She had to trust God to get them through this safely. And trust that Michael knew how to navigate this road.

Michael. He shouldn't be involved in any of this, and yet, again and again, they had found themselves in danger. Twice, she had attempted to strike out on her own, and twice, he had refused her offer. Now, after Aidan's threat to him, Michael was stuck with her. The painful truth was that, deep down, she was thankful, even as she knew she should beg him to leave her and find a way out of this danger. And yet, still, she couldn't fight how grateful she was that she was not alone.

"Hold on tight," said Michael. "It's going to be a little rough getting back on the road."

Ellie glanced behind them. They were out of the forest, in the open and higher up now, giving her a view between the cracks and crevices of the rocky hills. Behind them, a single light bobbed up and down over the white landscape. The snowmobile was gaining on them little by little.

"That has to be Aidan," she said. "The sled is still following us."

"How far?"

"Maybe a few hundred yards?"

"Not far enough. He's driving too fast for the area," muttered Michael. "Not a good sign."

Michael slowed as they approached the road, navigating around the jagged rocks that broke up the blanket of snow. Each time Ellie looked behind them, Aidan was closer.

"He has the faster vehicle, too," said Michael. "Once we get onto the road, I don't know how long I can keep him off."

"All we can do is try," she said. And pray.

Was Michael a man of faith? In those first months after Sean died, she had felt like she was drowning, like his death was pulling her under and keeping her there. Her belief had saved her life, and she hoped that Michael could feel God there with him, too.

"Hang on," said Michael as he drove them up the embankment and down the steep decline of the other side.

Above them, the mountain range ascended with a season's worth of snow clinging to the rocky face. In front of them, the two-lane road curved gently through the remainder of the valley then turned out of sight around a curve. The car tracks were barely visible in the new snow. Why weren't there vehicles on the road, now that the snow had let up?

"Just beyond that curve is where the road cuts through Angel's Slide," said Michael. "If we make it through that stretch, we can get off the road again."

Ellie didn't miss the *if* in that last sentence.

The snow glowed in the beam of the headlight, lighting a short distance in front of them and leaving the rest of their surroundings shrouded in darkness. They would move around the curves as the drop off the mountain grew steeper. They raced toward the first curve and then Michael cut the speed. As they rounded onto Angel's Slide, Ellie turned back and saw the light from Aidan's snowmobile flickering behind them, darting one way then the other. He was still gaining on them, faster now.

Michael slowed as they took the first corner then sped up as the road straightened. They dodged large chunks of snow that had fallen from higher up the mountain and rolled into the road. On her left, the mountain rose, and on her right, the edge of the road ended in a sharp drop into the canyon. The light from the snowmobile pursuing them dashed against the mountainside, and Ellie was afraid to check how close it was. If the sled caught them now, they could so easily be nudged off the road. Just one more hairpin turn.

"Hold on," said Michael. "Just after this turn, we'll get off road again."

She clutched Michael's jacket and braced herself. But as they rounded the corner, an enormous cloud of white blew toward them through the night air, overtaking them in a swirl of wind.

Ellie gasped as the cloud of powder enveloped them. *"Avalanche!"*

The gust of snow hit them, a white haze cutting off Michael's sight. He couldn't see the edge of the road and he couldn't see the wall of granite on the other side. At this speed, he could so easily kill them both.

"Lean in. We're turning," he called through the intercom over the noise of the storm.

Michael slammed on the brakes and made a U-turn into the lane of oncoming traffic, praying no one was coming toward them through the blinding cloud of white. He could barely see a few feet in front of him, but he had to get them closer to the mountain, away from the edge of the road. The snowmobile stuttered forward until they were now facing the way they'd come. The other sled would be rounding the corner at any moment. Michael couldn't count on Aidan—it had to be him—to turn back. He would be heading straight for them. But at their back was an avalanche, the force of it creating its own storm. He'd seen this before. A slide of heavier snow set off sandstorm-like winds that blew powder—and everything in its way—down the mountain. How close were they to the crushing river of snow? Would the heavier snow hit them from above, burying them alive? Or would they get blown right off the edge of the road? Danger lay in both directions. They were trapped.

Michael found the snowbank and pulled up to the base of the steep slope. Tiny flakes swirled while bigger chunks of snow pelted against his helmet.

"What do we do now?" called Ellie over the howl of the wind.

"We can't drive in this," Michael shouted through the intercom. "Not when I can't see."

The snow was already building over the skis of the snowmobile and covering them both in a white film.

"We need shelter," she called back.

But her words were drowned out by the roar of a snowmobile motor. *Aidan.* He was still pursuing them, and now he was at the hairpin turn. The single light flashed and bounced before it shone straight at them. Visibility was so low that whether he meant to or not, Aidan was going to hit their vehicle—and them—if they didn't get out of the way.

"Into the snowbank," bellowed Michael. "Now."

Michael scrambled off the snowmobile and grabbed Ellie's hand, and together they dashed through the new layer of blowing snow and climbed up the steep bank. Even just a few feet away, Ellie's figure was blurred through the storm.

The mountain was barely visible. Ellie's boots slipped through the powder, and Michael grabbed for her glove.

Protect her. Adrenaline raced through him as the message resonated in his entire being, strong and clear.

"Link arms with me so I don't lose you," yelled Michael. "I've got you."

Crack. The shatter of hard plastic against plastic, followed by the crunch of metal, echoed over the wind.

"Get down!" Michael called and then he threw himself on top of her, shielding her with his body as best he could.

Kernels of ice and bits of fiberglass pelted against him, so he held on tight to Ellie.

"Help us, Lord." Ellis's voice was a whisper in his ear, so quiet beneath the storm that he almost missed it. But it was there. She was praying, the way Sunny and he used to pray together.

"Amen," he whispered.

He waited for a breath, then another breath, until he was sure the spray from the collision had settled. Then he scrambled up and turned around, searching through the snow for Aidan. Pieces of black material, large and small, dotted the white landscape, scattered around the wreckage of both snowmobiles. Aidan—it had to be him—had slammed straight into their sled. One windshield had shattered and another dangled from the handlebar. The front skis were askew, and the front plates were in pieces all over the road. If he and Ellie hadn't jumped off in time…

Michael pushed that thought away and searched for Aidan.

"Do you see anyone?" he asked.

"Over there." She pointed farther down the road. "I see movement."

Michael whipped around and saw the faint figure in

the storm, the red coat glowing through the snow. Aidan lay in the snowbank, slowly lifting himself to sitting. It looked as if he had been thrown over the handlebars. The man was alive. That was all Michael needed to know to set him in motion.

"We have to get out of here," said Michael.

And it wasn't going to be on the sled. At least Aidan's snowmobile was in just as bad shape as theirs, if not worse. But this stretch of the road was far from everything, just rocky hills much too steep for anything other than parkland.

"We're only getting the powder part of the avalanche," said Ellie, "but who knows what's farther ahead."

"And the avalanche means that no one will be driving this way anytime soon," he added.

They were exposed out here on the mountain, and miles away from help. The snow was too deep to walk through for any length of time. All three of them would freeze out here if they didn't figure out something.

"I have an idea," said Ellie. She scrambled down the snowbank. "Grab one of these broken plastic pieces from the snowmobiles, something big enough to sit on."

She headed for the windshield lying in the road. Michael wasn't sure where she was going with this, but he had nothing to offer. Through the snow, he could see Aidan pushing up to standing.

"He's coming," Michael said as he jogged down the snowbank, following Ellie.

It was hard to find the pieces in the storm. His boot hit the front plate of his snowmobile, which had split in two. The side that had borne the brunt of the impact was shattered, but the other side was hanging off the vehicle mostly in one piece. Michael tore it off.

"We're going to use these as sleds," she said.

"Right here, from the side of the road?"

This stretch wasn't a sheer cliff, but it was steep and full of boulders. Also, the solid mass of the avalanche had hit somewhere close. They were on the edge of unsteady ground. If they strayed onto its path, he didn't want to think about what might happen.

What if Ellie didn't make it?

"It's too risky," he said.

"We're trapped. We have to get down the mountain to the— Look out behind you!"

Michael turned around and Aidan was right there.

The man went for his throat, but Michael held up the remains of the front plate like a shield, knocking Aidan's hand away. Michael threw his weight against the plastic piece, catching Aidan off guard, shoving him back.

The man's muffled voice made it through the wind, but Michael couldn't hear what he was saying. Last time Michael had caught Aidan off guard, but this time, he wasn't sure his wrestling moves would be enough. Ellie was right. The only escape was down.

Aidan lunged at him again.

"You go," he said through the intercom to Ellie. "I'll be right behind you."

"I told you I'm not leaving you."

Aidan's big body hit him, knocking them both to the ground. Above him, Michael caught a glimpse of Ellie as she brought down the edge of the windshield on the back of the man's leg. Aidan let out a yelp, and Michael rolled out from under him. He grabbed the front plate and scrambled to his feet.

"Go!" he shouted. "Please trust me."

Ellie hesitated and, for one long second, Michael thought she'd refuse. But then he heard her voice ring in his ears.

"You better be right behind me."

Through the blowing snow, he watched as she ran up the snowbank and disappeared into the darkness.

Michael kicked away the hand that grabbed his ankle and followed her up the mound. The swirling snow blocked his view, and all he could see was gray sky and a long and white blanket below him. There was nothing to do but pray and jump.

So he did.

TEN

Ellie flew over the blanket of snow, picking up speed on the steep mountain. She was curled up on the tiny Plexiglas windshield, her feet raised as she desperately held on to the curved sides. The new layers of powder didn't absorb nearly enough of the jostles and bumps from the rocks and logs and whatever else was buried under the snow. The more speed she gained, the harder she landed. The landscape rushed toward her in contours that came too fast for her to read. *Just a little farther.* She had to get away from Aidan.

Her heart kicked in her chest as the blur of white rushed by. She hadn't passed any trees yet, but there were some up ahead. How did she steer this thing?

And where was Michael? Was he right behind her, the way he'd promised to be?

Ellie pushed that thought out of her mind. She was gathering more speed at a frightening rate, and the faster she went, the more she wobbled and smacked against the buried landscape. She put her feet down in front of her, trying to slow the makeshift sled. The moment her heels hit the snow, the shield of her helmet was sprayed with a layer of white, making it impossible to see. She put her feet down further in the snow to stop herself, to wipe her mask, to figure out where she was, but suddenly she was airborne.

All her breath left her lungs as she flew through the air…
Tuck. Tuck now.

Her survival skills kicked in just as she hit the snow. Her left shoulder landed first, with a jolt, and then she was tumbling through the drift, curled up and rolling down the hill. She thanked the Lord for her helmet, even though it was still covered with snow, as she flailed and rolled, losing track of up and down. She needed to dig in somehow, to stop herself. Somewhere along the way, she'd lost the Plexiglas shield, so she stretched out her legs.

Thump. Whack.

Her leg hit something long and hard and her body jolted to a stop. Ellie's breath whooshed from her lungs as adrenaline coursed through her. Her leg was caught on something—a branch? She lifted her hand to wipe her mask, but before she reached it, a rush of snow rolled over her, burying her. Ellie tried to move her hands, her legs, but everything was stuck. She couldn't move. She was trapped. Her heart gave a fresh jolt of fear. She choked in a new breath as panic took over. She had to get out. Now. She tried to flail her arms, tried to kick, but after an inch of movement, her limbs were imprisoned by the coffin of snow. Her heart raced, and her breaths were short and fast, steaming up her visor. Was she going to suffocate here, buried alive?

This couldn't be God's will. No. It *couldn't* be.

"Help me!" she screamed, but her cry of desperation echoed in her helmet, deep under the snow. The helmet. It was why she had air, a little reprieve. How long would it last?

"Where are you, Ellie?" Michael's voice came through the intercom.

The intercom.

She could still talk to Michael. *Thank you, Lord, for bringing him to me.* His voice was a welcome comfort, a rock in the storm of panic that swirled through her. She reminded herself that she could breathe. That was something.

"I don't know where I am," she said, panting. "My visor was covered with snow, so I couldn't see what was happening. I fell off something and ran into something, I think a tree, and now I'm buried in the snow. I'm going to suffocate."

Ellie could hear the way her words came faster and faster, desperation leaking into her voice.

"I'm not going to let you die," said Michael, his voice firm and so determined that she believed it. She believed, against all odds, that he would help her. She had believed all her life that God would show her the way. Maybe this was her sign.

"I know you must be scared, but try to slow your breathing," continued Michael in that same reassuring tone. "I'm coming in your direction. Your fall must have let loose some of the snow from the tree or something, but I'll find you. I'll be there soon."

"How?" Was he just saying that to get her to calm down?

"So far, it's not too difficult. You left a trail."

"Are you making a joke?" She didn't know whether to laugh or to yell at him.

"I'm doing whatever it takes to get you not to panic."

"Me, too." She was trying so hard not to think about the heavy weight of the snow on her chest. How far under was she buried?

Ellie forced her thoughts onto something else. "What happened to Aidan?"

"He's probably right behind us. I'm guessing he'll find something to ride down the hill on."

He was still on their tail.

"One problem at a time, Ellie," Michael added.

"But there are so many to choose from."

Michael gave a dry laugh. Then all she heard was his breathing. How long would it take for him to find her? Did she have enough air—

"Whoa. You went off this? It's got to be almost twenty feet high." His voice was laced with both worry and amazement. "Are you hurt?"

Her shoulder was throbbing and her ankle was twisted in the branch.

"A little, but I don't think anything's broken," she said. "When I fell, my instincts from my horse-riding days kicked in."

"Okay. I'm heading down the side of... Wait—I see that windshield you were using as a sled."

Slow, deep breaths. *Give yourself over to God's plan.*

"I'm right here. I just need a little more direction from you," Michael said. "Tell me as much as you can about the tree where you got caught. How big does the branch feel?"

She moved a little. "I don't know. Maybe two inches thick?"

"Excellent. It sounds like you caught a lower branch, so the entire tree probably isn't buried. I just need to find it."

And fast.

"Keep talking," said Michael. "I need to hear that you're still okay. Tell me about your horse-riding days."

He was breathing hard, like he was laboring through the snow, and she tried not to focus on the fact that it was getting harder to breathe inside her helmet. Or the way the snow was pressing down on her chest. How long did she have? She searched her mind for something that was so far away from this moment. Something that was the opposite of being trapped.

"I grew up on a ranch in Northern California, right on the border of Nevada, and my parents... Well, it wasn't easy to make money. They loved me, but there was always something. But I had a horse. Buster. A palomino. During the summers, when I was out of school, I'd take Buster out around our land and help my dad mend the fences. I spent a lot of time on my own, and I loved it."

"So that's how you knew how to ride a horse. A true ranch girl," said Michael.

Ellie supposed she was, even after all these years living on the coast in Santa Barbara. It was funny that way, how she and Sean would go to events where the ballroom was filled with people, yet she'd felt so out of place that she'd been lonelier than she'd ever been on the ranch.

"One afternoon," she continued, "I was leading Buster down to the creek for a drink. As I stood there, I saw something move in this little space between a rock and a bunch of grass, just under a bush. I stood still, just watching, and sure enough, there was a nose. A rabbit hopped out. I watched it take another cautious hop, and then, from under the bush, I saw another tiny one. Then another and another poked their noses out. They were each small enough to fit in my hand." The memory brought comfort, so she kept going. "I've never seen something so beautiful, this little family, all out exploring together. I didn't want to get closer, to scare them and their mother, so I just stood there, watching for as long as I could. I would have stood there all day, but Buster snorted and they all disappeared again."

She could still see them, one jumping on the other's back, the third one nuzzling their mother's side.

"Sounds like…" Michael's voice trailed off and then he said, "I think I found the tree. I'm going to use my piece from the sled to dig, and I want you to tell me the moment you hear or feel any movement."

Her heart raced in her chest.

"See or feel anything?"

"Nothing."

"I'm moving, digging in a new place." She could hear his labored breathing and she wondered just how close he was to exhaustion. Her own body ached, and the place where she'd hit her head this morning throbbed from lying on it. The tips of her fingers were starting to cool.

"Still nothing?"

"No." What if he was at the wrong place? There was a chance he wasn't even near her. If she'd entered the more forested part, there were so many trees to choose from. The panic was building in her chest again.

Trust God. He has a plan. You've done everything you can. Now it's time to put yourself in God's hands.

Ellie took a deep breath.

"Thank you, Michael," she whispered.

He gave a humorless laugh. "Don't thank me yet."

"Thank you for being here for—"

Thump. Something hit her boot.

"That's it," she cried. "You hit my foot."

"Oh, thank you, God," whispered Michael. His voice held so much relief that she could hear how scared he'd been. He had been holding it in for her, protecting her. A rush of warmth spread through her.

The pressure of the snow on her body was easing. She could feel the weight lifting as he dug out her legs and then her torso, searching for the outline of her body. He found her arm and then…

Michael's voice came through the intercom. "What—"

And then he went silent.

"What—" The touch startled Michael, but he knew exactly who it was before he turned around. In his despair to locate Ellie, Aidan had fallen from the top of his mind. But their trail was too clear for the man not to find them, and Michael had felt the desperation, the determination in the way Aidan had fought him on the road at the scene of the crash. Ellie's brother-in-law was going to do whatever it took to get his way. His initial assessment had been right: this was a man who wouldn't hesitate to harm or kill someone. And right now, that someone was Michael.

He turned to face his attacker. Aidan had tossed his helmet off to the side, and his snarl of anger was mixed with a hint of smug satisfaction. It was the look of someone whose long-awaited victory had just arrived. Michael glanced down and saw where his confidence was coming from. Aidan's gun was pointed straight at him.

"This is perfect," the man gloated. "I couldn't have planned this better myself. It would've been a risk to kill you back at the house or on the road, but here?"

A gust of wind found its way down the back of Michael's neck. He had to get Aidan away from Ellie.

"Some animal will find you long before anyone else does and, by spring, there won't be anything left. Even if Ellie survives and finds her way back here, she won't stand a chance of convincing everyone that I had anything to do with your death. It'll be my word against hers. And who do you think people will believe? The businessman who has brought tax dollars to the area for the last twenty years, or the hysterical claims of a widow who barely sets foot in this county? I think I'll take those odds."

His words sent a chill through Michael. This man had thought it all through, and he didn't show any hesitancy to kill. They were right next to Ellie, still buried in the snow. Ellie, whom Aidan was planning to manipulate for the rest of her life—or until he found a way to take control of her share of the business. Michael wasn't going to let that happen. He needed a plan. In the meantime, he needed to keep this man talking and distance him from Ellie. He could just barely hear Aidan through his helmet, but there was no way he was going to take it off while the man was waving a gun around.

Michael put his hands up and took a step back, shuffling a bit to the side. The gun followed him.

"You are going to kill me and destroy your sister-in-law's life for your business?" he called to be heard through the helmet. Michael shifted again.

"Our whole life will collapse if we don't go forward," he said desperately. "The payments are piling up from the last project, and if we don't start with a new investment soon, we'll default on our loans. We'll lose everything, and that includes Elizabeth's Tahoe house, mine, my parents'. She's going to take us all down."

Another sharp gust of wind blew from the side and Michael pretended to stumble from its strength, moving farther away from Ellie. Out of the corner of his eye he caught her struggling out from under the snow.

"And if Elizabeth agrees to your terms, how can you assure her that she'll be safe in the future?" Michael asked.

"I have no reason to harm her if she complies," he said. Michael didn't know if he was telling the truth. "Unless she decides to go to the police. I'll hear about it right away."

That idea sent another chill through Michael. Ellie had been right when she'd said Aidan had friends on the force, people who would be loyal to him. If Aidan was willing to take such a risk, there must be some truth in it.

Michael saw Ellie tug her helmet off and gasp for breath. Relief coursed through him. She was free, and Michael had led Aidan away, step by step, so they were now a few yards from her. All she had to do was to grab the sheet of Plexiglas and start down the mountain. Chances were good that Aidan wouldn't hear her over the wind—not when the man was focused on Michael.

Get out of here, he silently begged her.

She didn't. Instead, she turned in his direction. Michael's stomach clenched and he saw her mouth set in a grim line of determination. She was going to get involved in this. Michael gritted his teeth, biting back the strong urge to warn her to flee.

"She'll need more than just your word as a guarantee," he said, keeping his eyes on Aidan.

"She's not in a position to negotiate. And neither are you."

Ellie was on her feet quicker than he would have guessed. As she stepped up behind Aidan, all of Michael's fears jumped to life.

"I'm right here, Aidan," she said.

As Aidan turned, Michael veered to the side. This was his chance. He grabbed the man's hand, pulling it toward the sky, but his glove made it impossible to wrench the weapon out of Aidan's grip. From behind, Ellie kicked Aidan in the knees and he collapsed forward. The gun went off, a deafening boom masking the howl of the wind.

"Are you hit?" Ellie yelled.

"No. You?"

"No."

"Grab your sled and let's get out of here," she shouted.

Michael glanced one more time at Aidan, struggling facedown in the snow. The gun was still somewhere with him, but Ellie was waiting. She held out the front piece of the snowmobile and, from the look on her face, she wasn't leaving without him this time. Did he struggle with Aidan for the gun, knowing Ellie would wait for him, risking another shot?

No. Not again.

He took the makeshift sled from her hand, hopped on it, and started down the mountain into the dark forest. As they descended, he heard a shot. Another one. Then a burning sensation pierced his side.

ELEVEN

The shots rang out down the hill, echoing inside Ellie with waves of dread.

"Are you hit?" she cried.

Michael didn't answer and it took her a moment to remember why. She had torn her helmet off the moment she had come out from under the snowbank, desperate to get air after she'd been trapped with it on. But that meant the intercom was gone. She could no longer talk to him.

The snow whipped at her face as she tore down the mountain. She glanced to the left then to the right for a glimpse of Michael, but the night landscape was a blur. And she knew better than to take her eyes off her path this time.

"Michael?" she called desperately into the darkness. All she heard was the wind howling up the mountain.

He should be right next to her, but she couldn't see anything. Maybe he was close behind her, following her trail again? She trusted him, trusted that he would do everything he could to stay with her. But what if his best wasn't enough?

Ellie had a very bad feeling about those two gunshots. They'd been at close range, and what she'd heard of Aidan's rant was more evidence that her brother-in-law wasn't afraid to kill. That much he had made clear.

That realization led to the thought that had been forming in the back of her mind since she'd left the house. Maybe *he* killed Sean?

It's your fault.

The flash came back from the cave, chased with the same crushing guilt that took her breath away. Aidan blamed her for Sean's death, and something about that had rattled her, something that was still stuck behind that hazy veil over her memories. But right now, she needed to focus on the forest in front of her.

Ellie put her feet down to slow herself for a turn and got a face full of snow, but the wind soon blew it away. She leaned to the side, dodging one tree, then another. She was getting the hang of steering her improvised sled, but she couldn't afford to make the same mistakes she had last time. Last time, her helmet had saved her. This time, she'd have nothing to protect her.

Her fingers were cramped from clutching the sides of the Plexiglas. Her legs ached. Her arms ached. Her rear ached from each bump she hit. Still, she continued down the mountain. She had no other choice but to keep moving as far away from Aidan as possible. If she didn't go, Michael wouldn't, either—which put him in direct danger.

Back at the fire tower, their plan had been to head to the ski resort. How close had they come when the avalanche had forced them off course? She had no way to navigate the forest except to continue down. Eventually she'd run into something…hopefully.

There was a break in the trees and she dug her boots into the snow. Another cloud of powder hit her face as she came to a stop in in the middle of some sort of trail. The snowfall had been heavy enough that the tracks were almost impossible to see it, but the trail was there, a perpendicu-

lar path through the forest. Maybe for cross-country skiing or snowmobiling? Her heart leaped in her chest. Maybe
this trail led to the ski resort, or at least somewhere public.

But where was Michael? Did she call for him? If he could
hear her, chances were good that Aidan could, too. Ellie
searched up the mountain for signs of him, but she couldn't
see anything. Instead, she found tracks heading down the
slope of the path. Very large animal tracks. Fresh ones.
The forest was alive around her, the snow swirling and the
trees bending and creaking in the wind. She stared down
the trail, looking for the animal that made those tracks but
it was too dark to see much of anything.

She was lost. Alone in the wilderness. So very alone.

"Trust your path," she whispered to herself. God had
been there for her in the cave. He had brought her to Michael at her lowest point. She needed to trust Him, even
when everything else around her didn't make sense.

Just keep heading down the mountain, she told herself,
away from the animal tracks. There was a river that ran
through the valley between the mountains with a road that
snaked along next to it. If there was a trail here, she'd run
into the road at some point. And hopefully she could find
a way to meet up with Michael there, too.

Ellie took one more look around her at the silent forest
then picked up the Plexiglas windshield, trudged across
the path, and brought herself to the edge of the slope. The
mountain continued down, disappearing into the night.

Trust Him.

She sat on the little shield, picked up her feet and let
herself go. She started slowly, but soon she picked up the
pace again, bounding down the mountain with enough
speed to glide over the flatter parts. Ellie tilted from side
to side, avoiding long-hanging branches as best she could

in the dark. She held on as the mountain took a dip then climbed. She came to a stop at the top of the incline. Far away through the trees, farther down the mountain, she could see the faint flash of red and blue lights skittering across the snow. Police lights.

Relief rushed through her first, but it was quickly followed by dread. Aidan knew the police around here, and she had no doubt that his word would be taken over hers. Still, if she got to the cops, maybe she could at least save Michael's life…if she could find him. So many *ifs*.

She had two choices. The direction of the ski resort, still not in sight, or the direction of the lights.

Please, Lord, show me the right path.

Ellie swallowed her dread and aimed herself down the hill, toward the flashing lights. It was a clear shot down to the road, so she let herself gain speed until she burst out of the woods and landed on the enormous, sloping bank next to a road. It had been plowed relatively recently, just a few inches of new snow on top, but it was quiet. To her right, the lights flashed in the darkness just beyond a curve in the road. To her left, the snowy road led to another bend and disappeared into the darkness. Did she try to find Michael or go for help?

She sat on the top of the snowbank, looking down at the Plexiglas below her. She had managed to get herself this far. She could endure whatever it took. As she sat there in the silence, catching her breath, she marveled at where the day had taken her. Back at the Green Living Construction office, she had cowered at Aidan's threats, even while she was determined to do the right thing. Now, she was no longer cowering. She was ready to face this head-on.

Ellie took a deep breath of the frigid mountain air. Her hair blew across her face. She should be cold by now, but her heart was pounding too hard for that. She would go by herself and face whatever this would bring her if it meant saving Michael.

Ellie scooted the snowbank, but as she stood, she heard a crack of branches behind her. Her heart leaped. *Michael*. He had made it down the hill.

She turned around, but it wasn't Michael she saw on the snowbank above her. It was Aidan, and he was coming straight for her.

Michael struggled to stay upright as the burning sensation shot from his side. Aidan's bullet had found him, and it felt as though there was nothing else in the world except for the pain. He shifted in his makeshift sled, trying to ease the aching, but he tipped over and tumbled through the snow. He put his hand out to stop himself from picking up more speed and he came to a stop. Slowly, he pushed to sitting. Next to him, the snow was tinted darker. Was that blood? How badly was he bleeding?

Dumb question. Any amount of blood here on the mountain could be fatal.

"Ellie," he called into the intercom. No answer. He called again. "Ellie? Where are you?"

Then he remembered. She had taken her helmet off in front of him and, for a while, he'd kept sight of her curly red hair flying down the mountain.

They were cut off from each other. He'd have to find her path and follow it. But just sitting up made his side throb angrily. He was in no condition to walk through the deep snow.

Their plan had been to reach the ski resort, but they weren't anywhere near it. Far, far below was the road that led to Clover Valley. Between here and the road? Just a few backcountry trails and lots and lots of wilderness. Now that she was out of sight, he had no idea how they would find each other.

Protect her, God. Keep her safe.

The drive to find her thrummed inside him, so strong. He told himself that she was not as vulnerable as she had been this morning when she'd jumped on the back of his horse, cold and panicked, but he still couldn't shake the feeling that every part of him wanted to protect her. Why did the thought of her in harm's way make his gut twist and his heart stutter with fear?

"Ignore it," he muttered to himself.

Right now, he needed to make it farther down the mountain, where he could put all of his energy into finding her. Protecting her. She was strong, but that didn't mean she didn't need support. And the two of them were safer together out here in the wilderness at night, with an angry and dangerous man chasing them. Of course he was worried about her, just like he would worry about anyone else. That's all this uneasy feeling in his gut was telling him. He wanted to be able to help someone the way he hadn't been able to help Sunny...

No, there was more to it.

He wanted to help Ellie because he couldn't bear the idea of her coming to harm, and the intensity of that want made the uneasy feeling worse.

Michael unzipped his jacket. The cold air burst in as he glanced at his left side. There was a hole in the fabric of his shirt and blood seeped through, bright and messy, an inch or two below his ribs. It seemed like the bullet had just grazed his side, but he couldn't do too much investigating here, out in the cold. Living on a ranch meant he'd seen his fair share of blood, enough that he guessed he wasn't in danger yet, despite the sharp pain that radiated from the wound. If he had any hope of finding Ellie, he needed to slow the bleeding as best he could. The hospital would have to come later.

He hadn't had the time to grab the backpack from under the seat of the snowmobile, so he was stuck without the first-aid kit. Maybe his neck gaiter? It would definitely be tight enough to apply some pressure to his side...if he could fit it over his shoulders. He shrugged off the coat and steeled himself against the oncoming pain it would take to get his gaiter onto the wound.

Michael grabbed the stretchy material with his right hand, trying to keep his left side as still as possible, and stretched the fabric as far as it would go. He tugged it over his left shoulder farther, farther, until it trapped his left arm against his side. He wedged his left hand under the bottom of the gaiter and pushed it up. He ignored the new slice of pain as he strained against the material. Was he stuck? Finally, he freed his arm, and the gaiter hugged the side of his chest.

Now he needed to get the gaiter over his other shoulder. He gritted his teeth and used his left arm to pull it down. Each move tugged at his wound, but he pulled and shimmied it down and pulled again until, finally, he slipped his right arm out, leaving the material stretched across his chest. Michael moved experimentally. It helped a little. And that had to be enough for now. It was the best he could do.

A branch snapped and he whipped around, wincing at the sudden movement. The noise had come from the right, close by, but a sizeable boulder blocked his view. Michael took off his helmet and strained to see farther, but the forest was silent.

"Ellie?" he said warily.

No answer. He had to keep moving.

Michael slipped his arms back into his coat and zipped it, trying not to use his left arm, then climbed back onto the front plate from the snowmobile and pushed off.

The mountain was steep enough that he picked up speed right away. Each bump from the buried landscape was a jolt, and each jolt shot a new spike of pain through his side. His vision grew dark around the edges. Michael tried to absorb the pain, tried to keep going, but the farther he went, the harder it was to sit up. Maybe he'd underestimated his injury.

Still, he clung to the plastic edges of his makeshift sled, continuing down the mountain, trying to watch for trees and rocks by the light of the moon and snow, farther and farther, until he came to a stop on a trail. Michael looked up and down the open path. He knew this trail. He and Aman had used it as a launching point for backcountry skiing. It started at the ski resort and ended at a parking lot by the side of the road that led to town.

Michael looked up the gentle slope, the path that led toward the parking lot, then down in the direction of the ski resort. The blanket of snow was marred by meandering tracks, and they didn't look human. There was no sign of Ellie…or of Aidan. That thought sent his heart pounding.

How far was he from the resort? He was getting weaker. Maybe his best chance was to get help from the resort…if he could make it that far.

"I won't fail you, Ellie," he said into the darkness of the night, as if speaking the words aloud would mean that God would hear him more clearly. As if it meant He would listen this time.

Michael turned his sled and pointed it toward the path. It was slow going compared to the mountain, but the smooth trail was a relief to his side.

But that relief was short-lived as the hairs on the back of Michael's neck rose. He wasn't alone—this time he was certain. He sensed someone. Something.

Michael turned, his torso complaining as he searched for movement. He saw nothing but snow. He thrust with his hands, gaining speed, peering into the darkness around him. His senses were on high alert. From below him, he heard a rustle, but the slope was too steep for him to go over the side of it. He pushed himself faster, searching the path in front of him for the glow of lights, but there was nothing. He was still miles from the ski resort.

A branch cracked somewhere below him, this time closer. Then he heard it: a low snort. It definitely wasn't a person. This was something else, and it sounded like it was close. Like it was following him. Michael searched his surroundings for something to protect himself with, but all he saw above him were tall trees and endless layers of snow.

Please help me find a way out of this.

Another snort came from behind him. Michael whipped around and his heart jumped. In his wake was an enormous black bear, and it was heading straight for him. The animal's head was low, its eyes fixed on Michael. It was stalking him.

TWELVE

"Where is Michael?" The question came out as her heart skittered in her chest. It was probably a tactical error, but Ellie didn't care. She needed to know where he was.

"I shot him," said Aidan so plainly and coldly. He stood above her on the snowbank, towering, his helmet under his arm. His cheeks were ruddy from exertion and the cold, and his hair was a slick, matted mess. There was no remorse in his voice, like he felt justified. Like Michael didn't matter.

"You shot a man," she said incredulously. "A person."

"Self-defense. And if he doesn't survive that?" Aidan shrugged, like it wasn't his problem. Like he had already thought this through and forgiven himself.

"Is he still alive?" she asked. Her voice shook as she tried to tamp down the panic that was rising inside her. *Please, not Michael, Lord*, she silently begged. Not another senseless death. Not the man who had stayed by her side throughout the most frightening events she'd ever faced. Not the man who had opened up to her about his own loss. Not the person she could understand, connect with. The idea of losing him so soon after he'd entered her life was too much to process.

"I'm more curious to hear *who* Michael is," Aidan said

with a snarl. "You two seem quite close. Especially for such a recent widow."

The sneer on his face was filled with anger and scorn. This man was even more dangerous and impulsive than she'd thought. Earlier, he'd had reasons to keep her alive, but those could flip at any minute. The more he found ways to fault her for his position, the less resistance he'd have to harming her. Ellie refused to tremble before this man, but she wasn't stupid. He had a gun. He had been pursuing her all day and, in his own words, he would never stop.

Right now, she had a choice between a man who was threatening her and the police, who very well might not believe her. The flashing lights weren't too far away, and the snow on the road could be measured in inches not feet. Ellie shuddered from the cold. If nothing else, the police had a warm, dry car. Maybe there was a chance that they'd send out a search and rescue team for Michael. This thought sparked a little burst of hope inside her. She had to find a way to talk Aidan down long enough to reach help. It was Michael's only chance.

"I met Michael today," she said. "He's no one. Just a stranger that stepped in when I needed help."

"I don't believe you."

Could he see on her face that this was both the truth and yet somehow a lie? There was something between them, something she had felt when he'd sat next to her at the fire tower. The connection felt nothing like friendship. She quickly pushed that dangerous thought away as she started down the road. Aidan quickly caught up with her.

He had pulled out his weapon. "I've been watching you," he added. "But you already know that."

Ellie stumbled as a sliver of a memory came back from the car ride home from the New Generation Construction meeting. Her phone. He had been using the location-sharing app on Sean's old phone to track her, which she'd understood as he'd crept closer in her rearview mirror. Moments after that realization, she'd lost control of the car. That was why she'd left her phone in the vehicle when she'd run. But it hadn't made a difference.

"I figured out why you ran down the mountain after you crashed your car," he continued. "You were trying to get to this man. You have him wrapped around your finger, just like Sean."

Ran down the mountain. The words rattled inside her, shaking out the memory of those moments after the car crash returned. Running through the snow, searching for someone who could help her, panic and confusion clouding her thoughts. She'd looked for a place to hide on the snow-covered mountainside, but Aidan had found her first and backed her into a cave. He'd yelled and lunged for her and then...everything was blank. She must have fallen, hit her head.

Ellie stared at him, stunned. Aidan had made her question her own mental state. Some part of her had wondered if his concern that she'd cause harm could be legitimate. But now that those last pieces of her memory had surfaced, she knew for sure that he had lied. What else would he do to get his way?

She forced herself to focus on what he'd just said to her. He was accusing her of manipulating both Michael and Sean—not good. He was going to jump to the worst possible conclusion no matter what she said. Aidan walked next to her, too close for comfort. She searched for a way to refocus him.

"What do you want from me?" she asked, trying to make herself sound conciliatory. "How do we end this?"

"First, if you decide to mention Michael or make up something about being forced against your will, then I'll make sure no one believes anything you say. You know how people feel about hysterical women. I'll let them know how much help you need. You do, you know."

Ellie couldn't believe all the things that were coming out of this man's mouth, but it was starting to dawn on her that he truly believed them. He saw himself as wronged by her.

"I'm not forcing you to do anything," he continued. "You manipulated Sean, and now you're trying to manipulate me. If you try to make my life harder, I'll do the same for you."

Talking him down really wasn't going well.

"So we head for the police and they take us into town. What happens next?" she asked.

"We go directly to the office, and you sign off on the next stage of building."

It was long after working hours, and the office would be empty. Ellie quaked at the idea of being alone with him. But Aidan needed her to do this. The details that had set off this whole disastrous chain of events this morning called out like a warning to her. Green Living Construction needed all three owners to sign off on expenses over five thousand dollars, and Ellie had to wonder why this clause had been in their rules in the first place. Had Sean or Clint suspected that Aidan wasn't trustworthy? Another shudder of dread ran through her as memories broke through that hazy cloud that still hung over her mind. Memories from this morning, inside the cave. Something to do with Sean. *It's all your fault.*

"Sean said no to your project," she whispered.

She hadn't meant to say it aloud, but it was too late. Aidan heard her, and his face exploded with rage.

"He backed out because of you. He said you wouldn't

want him involved in another project like the other one—the one where you're living. The one that you're still reaping the benefits from."

"I—I don't know what you're talking about," she stuttered.

"Liar."

There was so much frustration in his voice. Aidan definitely believed what he was saying. Had Sean used her as an excuse when he'd seen that Aidan was buying their way around laws and then written in the agreement clause about expenses? She wouldn't have wanted him to go forward after she'd seen the records of the "gifts" the company had given just before the committee's decision reversal...if she had known about it. But Sean hadn't said a word about it.

Your fault.

The accusation rattled her, the same way it had rattled her back in the cave. In a twisted way, it was true. Even if she hadn't had anything to do with it, she had wanted Sean to take a step back from the business that had sucked all his time, energy and attention. She hadn't wanted Green Living Construction to start on the next development because she had wanted her husband back. And now he was gone.

Should she have let it be? Should she have not pushed so hard? But that would have put strain on them in other ways. It would also mean that Sean could still be alive. Aidan needed to be stopped, but why had it had to come at the expense of her husband's life? The car crash was an accident, and there were so many if-onlys, too many to keep track of. If only they hadn't argued. If only they hadn't had an early snow that year. The cascade of ifs threatened to bury her, the way it had so many times.

Don't do this to yourself. It was in God's hands, not yours.

With that thought, relief came flooding through her. It wasn't her fault. A new thought occurred to her, one that, up until this point, she hadn't let herself think. Another if-only. If only Aidan hadn't followed him that day.

"You were behind him. At the car crash."

"I wasn't chasing him," he snapped, as if her words had been an accusation. "I just wanted to talk more. Our discussion wasn't over."

The words sent a new wave of fear through her. She could read between the lines, hear what he was denying. The brothers had had an argument and Aidan had been upset with Sean. Did Aidan, deep down, blame himself, too? Ellie wasn't even sure he'd let himself think that far. It was easier to blame her than to blame himself.

This conversation was getting worse. She picked up the speed as they continued down the road toward the curve. Everything she said seemed to anger him more, making him even more volatile. As they rounded the curve in the road, she strained to see the police car.

We're in God's hands. The thought was a balm for her. Not only couldn't she change the past—she needed to stop blaming herself. She needed to let it go. She had done her best with what she'd known, but God decided, not her. Not even Aidan. Just like He decided right now.

She caught the first glimpse of the police car up ahead. This was nowhere near over, but Ellie was ready for whatever she would face next.

The police car was parked at a quiet intersection, blocking the road in the direction Ellie and Aidan came from. Two officers stood underneath the dark traffic light, dressed in thick jackets and winter hats. As Ellie came closer, she could make out one as a tall man standing in the middle of the intersection. The road seemed to be blocked off to traffic—maybe because of the avalanche? The other officer was shorter, with her long hair tied in a low bun. She stood next to the only other vehicle in sight, talking to the driver through the window.

"I'll do the talking," said Aidan in a low voice. "Don't try to manipulate this situation. Remember, if you ruin my life, I'll ruin yours."

As the mix of frustration and bitterness came through in his voice, Ellie shivered. This was a man who had just shot Michael, and left him out on the mountain, and now he was talking about her ruining his life? Aidan was both single-minded and determined, and she could feel that he was never going to leave her alone. Ever.

When this day had started, the crime Aidan had committed was bribery, the kind of crime that he could just pay more money to smooth over. But shooting someone? Ellie wanted to think that there were bigger consequences for that, like jail. But Aidan's plan was to deny all of this, and he seemed to have enough confidence in this scheme that he was walking by her side, straight for the police. What other crimes had he committed? A shot of fear ran through her. She had celebrated Christmas with him, sat next to him *in church*. She had to be careful. Unless they found Michael, there was nothing concrete to show the police that Aidan was a threat to her.

Before, her intention had been to retrieve the go bag and run, but now she was no longer just choosing for herself. She had to consider Michael in her strategy, too. If she opened up to the police right now, and they didn't believe her, it would provoke Aidan, putting her and Michael in even more danger. That was especially likely if her brother-in-law knew one or both of the officers. Then again, what other choice did Ellie have? Michael was injured up on the mountain. That was more important than escaping Aidan right now.

Please, Lord, let him live.

Ellie walked through the snow as exhaustion churned with fear inside her. Each step was more difficult than the last. She had been running all day, and the urge to surrender, to give up this fight, was strong. She wanted to rest, and maybe, if it was just her, she might have given up. But Ellie needed to know that Michael was safe, and that need overpowered everything else. She had to try.

So she straightened, refusing to give in to fear, as they rounded the police car and stepped into the intersection. The lone car drove away, leaving the four of them standing in the snow, the flashes of blue and red lighting up their faces. The woman was closer, but Aidan ignored her.

"Garrett," he called in that hardy confident voice, so different from the snide bitterness he'd used with her.

Ellie's gut twisted as the worst-case scenario came true. Aidan did know the officer, and he was using the same voice she'd heard him use too many times before, that charm of someone who was confident that life would go his way. And this was a friend. The chances of the officer believing Ellie over him had just dropped precipitously.

"Aidan, buddy, is that you?" said the officer, his voice full of concern. "What are you doing out here in the storm? Did you get stuck in the avalanche?"

"We got caught on the edge of it and wrecked our sleds up on Old Mill Road," he said. "Barely made it out of there."

Garrett turned to the other officer. "Hey, Renee? You direct for a while. I'm going to get these two something warm to drink."

Ellie's heart sank further as she heard the tone the man used to talk to the woman. Clearly, he was in charge—or at least he assumed he was. This situation was going to get worse if she didn't act fast.

"Officer, Aidan shot at a man up on the mountain, and I'm afraid he's going to die up there. Can you please call a search and rescue team to find him?" She said it loud enough for both officers to hear, hoping for support from the woman.

Garrett looked at Aidan, but he just lifted an eyebrow at Ellie and shook his head. His expression was baffled, as if he didn't have the slightest clue what she was talking about.

"What is she talking about?" Garrett asked Aidan.

Frustration bubbled inside her. How could this man turn to Aidan for an explanation instead of her?

Aidan tilted his head a little, giving her a patronizing smile, then turned to Garrett. "Can I have a word with you in private?"

"Of course."

Of course? Ellie's heart rate kicked up even further as she watched them both turn their backs on her. She could see how effective Aidan's strategy was, hinging on the trust of a personal relationship and probably the man's subtle instinct that she was less reliable. He was going to distract and mislead, and bury this long enough for Michael not to survive. It was so unjust that her growing frustration threatened to overwhelm her. The only thing stopping her from yelling was that it would almost certainly be one step backward from saving Michael. Ellie tamped down her anger and focused on getting both officers' attention.

"Officer Garrett, Officer Renee, Aidan is going to tell you that I'm delusional, that the death of my husband is making me unstable. He's been pursuing me all day long, and he's trying to silence me."

Even as she spoke, she could hear she was losing ground

with the officers, not gaining. Especially since she'd approached them with Aidan at her side. To their ears, this might sound like their definition of crazy. Even yesterday, she never would have thought all that had taken place today was possible.

"Please, Officers," she said, trying to calm her voice. "I'm speaking the truth, but you don't even have to believe me. All I'm asking is for you to send a team into the mountains. There's a man up there who needs a rescue team. Please. Send someone to help him."

Garrett gave her a patronizing smile. "Of course we'll investigate this. Right now, we need to direct traffic, but when the storms over, we'll—"

"He doesn't have that kind of time," she snapped and then turned to the woman. "Please, Officer. Just call this in. Send someone up there."

The woman looked uncertainly from Ellie to Aidan to Garrett, as if she wasn't sure what to do next.

"She's a little out of sorts, but that's understandable," said Aidan, giving her a smile masked as kindness. "It's been a rough day. Perhaps if she warms up a little, that will help things?"

Ellie felt as though she were sinking in quicksand. The more she struggled, the more entangled she became in this quagmire Aidan had set for her. That was why he'd so confidently walked toward the police, despite the fact that he'd just shot a man. He'd known he could do this. Had he done something similar before? That thought sent yet another chill through her. She couldn't give up.

"Why don't we call another squad car to take you back to the station?" said Garrett.

The man put his hand on her shoulder to lead her to the police car. She had the strong urge to shake off his arm, get away from him, but that would only mire her even deeper into the quicksand. She fought against the feeling of helplessness.

As Garrett opened the door, Aidan's voice came from behind her. "Thank you for understanding. I'll call my foreman to pick me up."

Ellie froze, her hand on the door. He was calling his foreman, one of the men who had come to Tang Ranch for her. Aidan wasn't calling for a ride; he was calling for backup. Would they return to the mountain to find Michael? Ellie shivered and forced herself to climb into the car. The female police officer came to the door.

"Would you like some hot chocolate?" she asked quietly.

Ellie nodded. "Thank you."

The woman unscrewed the cap of a thermos and gave her a sympathetic look, though it didn't change the situation. Even if this woman believed her and wanted to help, she would be overruled by the guy who was in charge. Aidan's friend.

The woman poured the steaming drink into the plastic mug, handed it to Ellie and walked away. Ellie sat in the police car, gulping the hot chocolate and trying to figure out what to do. Her fears had come true. No one had believed her—no one except Michael. And now Michael was somewhere on the mountain. Was he injured…or worse? Ellie didn't want to consider that possibility. Especially since she was stuck there, waiting for Aidan's henchman to come and the squad car Garrett had called to arrive—with officers who would take her back to the station while Michael was out somewhere on the mountain. *No.* She couldn't sit and let this happen. She had gotten him into this mess and it was her responsibility to get him out.

The police car was parked at the T in the road. To the left

was the road to town, the road the squad car would use to arrive and then take her back into town. It was where the two officers now stood, talking to Aidan. Straight ahead was the road that followed the mountainside. It wove back and forth, and eventually came up…somewhere. She didn't know where, so that wasn't a good option. The only direction that held any hope was behind her, the road to the resort. If Michael had somehow made it off the mountain, then maybe their original plan could work: connect there, lose Aidan in the anonymity of the hotel, and then, with the help of Michael's friend, escape. And if Michael hadn't made it? The image of him shivering in the cold was a punch in the gut. The pain was physical, and her whole body grew weak under her.

"You just met him this morning," she whispered to herself. "You barely know him."

But those last words didn't feel right. She cared about him, much more than she would have thought possible after just one day… Wariness took over as these thoughts ran through her, thoughts she didn't know what to do with. Because she wasn't going to fall for Michael. She wasn't capable of falling for anyone.

So Ellie pushed the thoughts out of her mind and refocused on her current situation. There must be a search and rescue team somewhere, or at least a snowmobile she could rent to search the place herself. The only hope of finding him was to follow the road. The problem was to leave the police car without anyone seeing her.

Ellie stared out the window at Aidan and the two officers, the three figures lit by the flashes of red and blue from the light bar on their car. They stood with their backs to her, about twenty feet away, talking in low voices. When Aidan turned to make a comment, she could see glimpses of that smile of his—confident and yet asking for sympathy. How many times had he done this, covered up his bad behavior with this friendly polish? She was not going to let him do it to her again.

The trick was to slip off quietly when they were turned away. She hadn't been arrested, so there was no reason she couldn't leave... Ellie took one more gulp of the hot chocolate, letting the liquid warm her insides and gathering her energy, then screwed on the lid.

She slid over to the driver's seat on the far side of the car and reached for the door handle. Ducking down, she cracked open the door and slipped out into the night, staying low. Their voices were still quiet, and she hoped that meant they hadn't seen the light from inside the vehicle. Gently, she closed the door and then ran as fast as she could for the curve in the road. Her boots clomped on the snow-covered pavement, and she tried to swallow back her gasping breaths.

"Elizabeth." Aidan's voice carried over the snowy road, but she didn't turn around. Would the police follow her? She couldn't rule it out. All she could do was look ahead and run.

Her legs felt heavy and clumsy as she made her way through the snow, and her boots slid under her feet, but she didn't stop. She headed for the curve. Still no sound above her gasping for breath.

"Elizabeth. Come back here."

As she rounded the first curve, Aidan's voice grew quieter. She turned around for a last glimpse at the scene behind her. The two officers stood in the intersection, watching her. But halfway between the police car and her, Aidan was following on her heels.

Ellie's heart stuttered in her chest. He was pursuing her,

and all that stood between them was her endurance, which was already stretched thin. How far was the ski resort? Did she have the strength to make it to there on foot?

She would if there was any hope to help Michael. And the police weren't following her, so she still had a chance. That thought gave her a little push as she ran into the night, along the empty stretch of road, trying not to look back again. As she passed the spot where she and Aidan had emerged from the mountain, a new thought occurred to her. Would he shoot her? So far, he had wanted her alive, but maybe he would do it and call it self-defense? It was hard to do that when you put a bullet through someone's back, but sadly, it wouldn't be the first time people bought that argument. Also, the police had just seen them together. Ellie hoped that would be enough to make Aidan think twice about shooting her.

The glow of the police lights faded, but ahead, in the distance, she heard the heavy hum of an engine. She came to another curve and, as she rounded it, white lights flashed in front of her. There was a mound of snow in the middle of the road, taller than she was, and two bulldozers slowly working to shovel it. The avalanche.

She ran toward it. One worker stood to the side of the frozen stream of snow, directing people through a walkie-talkie. As she approached, the man flagged her down.

"Hey. No crossing here until we clear the road."

Ellie ignored him and started up the mound of chunky snow.

"Hey!" The man's voice was sharper this time. "You're not supposed to…"

The rest of his sentence, faded, drowned out by the bulldozer coming at her.

Ellie scrambled to the side, dodging machinery, and continued over the snowbank, her heart pounding. Her legs ached and burned, but she couldn't stop. She used her hands to climb over the blocks of snow. It was hard, dense, the opposite of powder, but the ripples and bumps made the surface too uneven to run. She glanced behind her and saw Aidan standing on the top of the mound. Much too close, and the resort wasn't in sight.

"I promise you, Michael. I won't stop," she whispered to herself.

Finally, she hit the road again. She climbed off the avalanche's flow and sprinted toward the lights that glowed from just beyond the curve of the road. The resort. It was close. Ellie stumbled, her feet dragging through the snow, but she caught herself with her hand, picked herself up, kept going.

"You know you can't run from me, Elizabeth." Aidan's voice sounded much too close. "Who will people believe— you or me? I'll have you committed if that's what it takes to get you to do what's best for our company. You know I can do it."

Ellie tried to shut out his words, but that feeling of resignation was strong. She couldn't run for the rest of her life. He'd keep pursuing her until he got his way. The reality of that stretched out in front of her like slow suffocation, and her legs begged her to give in.

Maybe that was true, but Michael was still out there on the mountain. She wasn't going to let Aidan corner her until she found Michael. She couldn't lose sight of that purpose.

Ellie continued around the curve until the resort was in front of her. As she ran, she took in the layout, assessing it, trying to come up with a strategy. The place was a sprawling chain of buildings at the bottom of the mountain, with a main lodge, built in a large, log-cabin style, to welcome the guests. The hotel spread out like wings on both sides, with two taller buildings and then a series of smaller cabins tucked away into the mountainside. Behind the main lodge, a little village of shops and restaurants was just in sight, climbing into the mountain, and behind the shops, the chairlifts spread in different directions up the mountain. Most were dark, but a string of gondolas seemed to float above the snow, toward the lights of a building near the peaks.

If she could get inside the hotel, she could run up the stairs, lose him on the floor, maybe duck into someone's room while she called security. All she needed was a locked door to buy her some time. Or maybe she could convince housekeeping to let her in? The problem was how to get some distance from Aidan, to find a way he couldn't follow her and sabotage anything she tried. She had to figure out how to ditch him somewhere.

She glanced behind her. Aidan had slowed to a walk, but his dark figured was menacing.

She was close, so close. The outside of the resort was quiet. With the road blocked, no cars were visible at the entrance. Two doormen stood outside the sliding-glass doors as she ran toward the circular drive. The taller man gave her a wary look.

"Can I help you with something, ma'am?"

Ellie tried to paste on a smile and shook her head. "No, thanks."

She needed help, but Aidan would probably get any information she gave them. At this point, she was on her own.

"Stop that woman," called Aidan from behind her.

Ellie didn't wait to see if the doormen were going to listen to Aidan. She slipped through the door and darted into the lobby, scanning the place. Guests lounged on the overstuffed sofas and sipped their drinks, as if the last thing on their minds was running for their lives. To her left was a hallway, so she took a chance and turned into it, passing the empty concierge counter. She sprinted to the end, where the hall turned to the right. She found herself in a wider hall, with signs by the doors that said Conference Room A and Conference Room B. She glanced at one then the other, then headed for B.

"Where did the woman with the red hair go?" Aidan's voice echoed through the empty hall.

Ellie rested her hand on the long door handle and pulled down. The handle moved and the door opened into a dark room. Ellie froze as the sliver of light gave her a momentary glimpse of dozens of circular tables covered in white tablecloths. At the other side of the room was a doorway. An escape. She quickly stepped in and let the door click shut, plunging her into the darkness.

"Elizabeth?' Aidan's voice taunted her from the other side of the door. Her heart jumped in her chest as she started around the perimeter of the dark room. She held out her right hand, letting touch guide her along the wall. She reached her other hand out ahead of her, feeling for obstacles. A soft yelp of surprise escaped her lips as her left hand brushed against something in front of her. A table, she thought as she inspected it further. She used her hands to feel her way around, then shuffled forward until she reached the corner. As she turned left, pointing herself in the right direction, the main door she had come through opened behind her and the room lit up again. She whipped around as her heart thumped that familiar pattern of fear in her chest. There, in the doorframe, was Aidan. Her body froze and stars dotted her vision. He was closing in, and the panic was creeping through her.

No. She would not let this happen. Instead, she tamped down her fear, turned toward the rear door and sprinted. Aidan was after her, on her tail, as the light faded from the open door then disappeared. They were in the dark. His breaths filled the room, panting as he followed her. *It's a straight shot to the door*, she told herself. *Just keep going.*

There was a sound, a thump, and Aidan muttered a curse. The table? He must've run into it.

Ellie continued forward, keeping one hand on the wall until she felt the indent from the door. She moved her hand up and down, grasping for the handle, until she found it. She opened the door and light flooded the room again. As she sprinted out, she caught sight of Aidan charging after her.

Ellie scanned the hallway she was now in, too quiet and empty. The rooms were numbered—meeting rooms or guest rooms? She ran by them, pounding on the doors, but no one opened them. She yelled for help, but no one answered.

Aidan burst out the conference room door, and she sprinted for the end of the hall, to the exit outside. The cold air hit her as she ran into the snowy night.

In front of her was what looked like an old-fashioned mountain village. Quaint buildings lined the snowy paths, strings of lights hanging from the awnings. Ellie ran down the pathway, scanning the businesses, trying to find one to hide in. A candy shop, an upscale clothing store… She came to a stop in front of an Italian restaurant, pulled open the door and rushed inside. Then she halted. Bad choice. The clientele, who had been quietly eating, were now staring at her as she panted.

The hostess with a blond ponytail and impeccable makeup plastered on a smile and raised her eyebrows. "Table for one?" she asked skeptically.

Ellie scanned the room. "May I use your bathroom?"

The woman gave her a slow nod and gestured toward the back of the restaurant. Ellie took off, dodging tables and almost tripping over a woman's fur-lined boot. She was making a scene, exactly what she shouldn't be doing.

The restroom sign pointed down a little hallway. Ellie took one more glance at the front door then headed down the dimly lit passage, praying that this would work. But when she opened the door to the women's bathroom, she could see this, too, had been a mistake. There was no lock on the main door, and the doors to the four stalls started at her knees. She couldn't hide there. She ran out into the shadowed hallway, but when she emerged into the dining room, her heart stopped. Aidan was standing at the entrance to the restaurant, looking straight at her.

She met his gaze, saw the bubbling rage in his eyes that he barely held under control. She glanced around the restaurant. Conversations had stopped. Everyone was looking either at him or at her. Ellie swallowed. The only exit was in the front, right next to where he was standing. She looked behind her. It was just the doors into the kitchen. Maybe there was a way out there? It was her only hope. With one more glance at Aidan, she took off toward the double doors and burst through them. The kitchen was all fluorescent lights and stainless-steel counters. No one even looked up as she ran in. She passed a sous chef, chopping carrots, and a line cook, sautéing something over a flame as oil spit from the pan.

All Ellie needed was the door, and then…and then what? Aidan's voice echoed inside her. *You can't keep running.* How would she find help for Michael when she couldn't get him off her tail?

She looked one way then the other. On one side was the

enormous silver door to the cooler. But where was the door to the outside? There had to be one here…

The double doors burst open again and she didn't need to look to know who it was.

"Clear the kitchen!" Aidan announced. "This woman is dangerous."

She was trapped. And Aidan was here for her.

THIRTEEN

Michael stared across the white expanse at the black bear that growled and snarled at him. Its slick dark coat gleamed against the snowy landscape, and it was large, larger than the bears he'd seen before… Or maybe it was just closer. The animal's brown muzzle drew attention to sharp rows of teeth, and its small, close-set eyes were focused directly on Michael.

No one wanted to face a hungry bear in the middle of a forest. Especially not when the person in question was bleeding.

Michael had seen a handful of bears as they'd lumbered across the ranch, scaring the animals while scavenging for food, but most of the time, they'd stuck to the new developments, where the weekenders lived. It was yet another problem with the new development: part-time residents who still hadn't gotten the hang of keeping their garbage locked up. Black bears used to hibernate in these parts, but the steady diet of garbage kept them awake longer and longer, until they'd started to stay out year-round. But that didn't mean that they had enough to eat. At this point in the winter, after five months of steady snow, their forest diet was still buried. This was the time of the year when animals got desperate.

The bear's gaze fixed on Michael, focused and intent. This must have been what he'd heard farther up the mountain while he'd tried to staunch the bleeding from his side. He'd pushed the rustling he'd heard out of his head due to more immediate concerns—like the fact that he was in the middle of the forest with a bullet wound on his side—but now, the worst possibility his mind had flitted over had come true. The bear had caught a whiff of blood and stalked him.

It took another few steps closer, sniffing the air and snorting.

Michael stood absolutely still, trying not to panic, trying to think through the situation. It was too late to debate whether he would meet the bear's gaze or not—they were staring at each other. Michael's heart raced as his mind jumped through his options. Though he could hear the faint grumbles of a snowmobile and maybe a plow in the distance, they were too far away to be of any help. His instinct was to run, to head for the forest, climb a tree, somehow get some distance, but that was a terrible strategy. First of all, bears were great climbers, much more agile than Michael, especially considering the wound at his side. Also, running changed this into a game of chase, which he definitely didn't want. The only real option was to stand his ground and try to scare the bear away. It was a long shot, but it was the only thing he had.

The trick was to show greater strength, to make the bear think it didn't have the advantage, that it was going to lose this standoff. If it worked, even just to stall, Michael could slowly back away. This would have been a little easier without the scent of blood Michael was carrying, but he was going to fight despite the odds.

He needed to be taller and louder than this bear to have

any hope of carrying out his plan. Slowly, Michael bent down and grabbed the front plate of the snowmobile, the one he'd been using as a sled. It wasn't big, but it was better than nothing, so he lifted it over his head. His wound throbbed at the movement, and he tried to ignore it. Stretching was one of the worst things he could do for his side, but it wouldn't matter if he didn't make it through this.

Michael started talking calmly. He prayed for help aloud, talking to Him about his fear of the bear. The bear stopped. The animal remained focused on him but was no longer advancing, so he kept talking. And he found himself talking to Ellie.

"I'm coming to find you, Ellie," he said. "I won't let you down. I'll be there for you."

He gave out more promises, which he hoped he had a chance to fulfill. Somewhere in the back of his mind, as he waved and talked, it occurred to him that he was fighting for his life. Just this morning, he had been buried so deep in his grief that he couldn't see his way out. But now, with the bear in front of him and Ellie somewhere, struggling on her own, it was quite clear how much he had to live for. He had his family, he had the ranch and, today, he had Ellie. He wanted to live this life so badly. Why did it have to take this for him to realize it?

The Lord works in mysterious ways.

The answer came to him in Sunny's voice. This had been at the center of their conflict in the months before she died. She had accepted the path in a way that had sometimes even angered Michael—why hadn't she fought harder?

But right now, as he called out into the forest, with the bear staring at him, Sunny's message was what he needed to hear. *Live the life the Lord has given you*, Sunny told him, somewhere deep inside him. *Live this life, wherever it takes you.*

The bear still hadn't moved, so Michael stepped back, testing the animal. The bear stepped forward, shooting another spike of fear through him. No amount of survival skills could overpower the scent of Michael's blood. The animal headed straight for him, so he did the only thing he could think of. Michael poured out his heart.

"I'm not leaving the ranch," he said to his parents, miles away. "I'm sorry. I know that hurt you for me to say it, but I couldn't see a way to stay. But now I can. I want to be there for you. I want to honor our family."

It felt so good to say that, a relief, despite the bear's moving closer and closer. It was only ten feet away now. Michael's side burned, but he swung the front plate, ready to fight. Because, despite the fact that he would never get over losing Sunny, he wanted to live. He wanted to experience the joy that there was in life, even knowing that sorrow was there, too. He wanted to experience that with Ellie.

"Sunny, I miss you. I will never stop missing you. And nothing will change that."

He wasn't sure who he was talking to anymore. Was he talking to God? These were the things that he had buried deep in his heart, when the suffering had felt like too much. But now they were coming out.

His mind registered a snowmobile wailing in the background, and it was getting closer. Had someone heard him? Were they looking for him? The bear was approaching, its eyes hungry, its mouth open. The snorts came from inside the animal, deep and threatening.

The bear continued forward, growling. Michael took a swing with the front plate then doubled over in pain. The bear stopped. Then the animal reared up on his hind legs and growled. It must have been six feet tall, Michael's height, but it had a few hundred pounds on him. Even under the best conditions, there was no way that he could fight off the bear with a piece of plastic, and these were far from the best of conditions. But he was going to try.

He swung his shield again, and the bear batted it away, out of his hand. Now it was just him and the bear, facing each other. If this was the way Michael was going to die, he wasn't going down without a fight. Somewhere in the back of his mind that thought clicked together with his tangled-up feelings about Sunny: the guilt that plagued him was tied up in his grief. He had wanted her to fight harder.

Through the pain of that thought, he had a hard time registering the roar of a motor coming up from behind him. Then the noise clicked and he glanced over his shoulder. A snowmobile stopped right behind him. A driver in a ski patrol jacket motioned to him.

"Get on."

She didn't have to tell him twice. Michael jumped on, ignoring the screaming ache from his side, and the snowmobile started forward, away from the bear and into the forest. Michael turned and caught a glimpse of the bear lumbering after them, but they were moving far too fast for the animal.

Thank you, Lord. This time he prayed with meaning. For the first time in years, he felt thankful. Despite the awful turns of the day, there was something to be thankful for. And in that prayer, a glimmer of his old self reawakened, the man who was thankful for what he had. His gratitude had pulled him through many of the difficulties and injustices of the world. He had thought this part of him was dead forever, but here, despite his fear of yet another loss, he was thankful.

Michael held on to the stranger as the snowmobile rattled underneath him. He had never noticed how much these machines shook until now, when he felt every vibration in his aching side. He could barely keep his left arm up, let alone hold on. The adrenaline of coming face to face with the bear was fading, and the cold, the loss of blood and the pain were all setting in.

Everything inside him wanted to ask this driver to just pull over and let him sit for a while, but he refused to give in. Not when Ellie was somewhere out there on the mountain—or worse.

The driver followed the path down the slope of the mountain through the deep snow. The wind whipped icy flakes at Michael's face as he searched for tracks, for some sign of Ellie as they descended. The avalanche storm had coated the trees in white, thicker and thicker, until they came to a mound of chunky snow that covered the path. The driver brought the machine to a stop, letting the motor idle.

She pulled off her helmet and turned around. She had short, brown hair and penetrating brown eyes. Across her nose was a spray of dark freckles. "You okay?"

Michael didn't even know where to begin with that question. "I'm alive. Thanks for that."

"You didn't have much time left," she said. "I thought bears generally left people alone."

Michael wiped the melting snow from his face. "They do, but I smell like blood." He pointed to the hole in his jacket. "I was shot."

The woman's mouth dropped open. Then her gaze turned wary, like she was no longer sure she should have picked him up.

"I don't have a gun," he added.

The woman nodded and the lines on her forehead smoothed

a little, but the alarm hadn't left completely. "Hunting accident? Or something else?"

Michael searched for a way to explain the situation that didn't sound so outrageous. Ellie's appearance on his property, the amnesia, the go bag, the fight in Ellie's house… Yesterday, if someone had told him what this day would look like, he would have laughed at them. Michael felt a flash of sympathy for Ellie. It was no wonder she'd been so hesitant to tell him—or anyone—about her situation.

Still, he had to try.

"Someone is chasing a woman I…" Michael swallowed. "A woman I care about. I'm worried she's out here, alone in the wilderness somewhere, with the man who shot me. We have to help her."

The woman blinked at him like she had no idea what to do with this information.

"Please," he added. "This is really important."

"You're bleeding," she said. "You need to go to the hospital."

Michael shook his head. "First, I need to make sure she's okay."

The woman just stared at him. Was she going to overrule his request and do what she thought was best? Ellie didn't have time for him to go to the hospital.

Slowly, her eyebrows raised. "Look, I was almost caught in the avalanche, so when I heard you calling, I couldn't ignore it. I had to help. But do you hear what you're asking me to do? I have a family."

Michael blew out a breath. He did understand. He had a family, too. A family he'd been taught from birth he needed to care for, to honor. A family that would give up everything for him. Parents who had made sacrifices for him. Michael bowed his head. He didn't want this woman to get hurt. Michael searched for another solution, but his mind was hazy.

"Will you take me to the resort hotel?"

The woman hesitated then nodded.

Maybe he could find Aman. At least he could leave a message at the desk and borrow a snowmobile. Or send out some sort of search party.

"I'm Michael, by the way," he said. "I'd shake your hand, but I'm trying not to move."

"Cassie," said the woman. "Still debating whether it's nice to meet you."

"Thank you for coming," he said then quirked up the corners of his mouth. "It's definitely nice to meet you."

As Cassie smiled back, the conversation echoed in his mind, not so different from the one he'd had with Ellie this morning. How quickly he had gone from rescuing someone to needing rescue himself.

Cassie put on her helmet, gunned the engine and then started down the hill. They drove along the mountain through the snow, skirting the edge of the trail the avalanche had left behind.

As Michael clung to his rescuer, his mind drifted again to Ellie. It felt impossible that they had met *this morning*. Then again, today, the two of them had been through enough that he… Finishing that thought scared him. It would be disloyal to the woman he loved. His wife. The woman he had planned to spend the rest of his life with. The woman who was gone now. What would she say?

He knew what Sunny would say. She had told him her biggest hope was for him to live a full life, to work hard, to make his parents proud, and maybe even fall in love again. She'd wanted him to have all the things that they had wanted together. She'd said those words, but at the time he hadn't been able to ever imagine life without Sunny, let alone wanting to spend it with someone else. But something had shifted in him today. He could feel new possibilities open inside him, though these feelings were too new for him to process.

Why now? Maybe he already knew the answer. He had lost so much. Every decision he'd made these last two years was to protect himself from more loss. Now here he was, facing danger after danger. But he didn't have the urge to retreat the way he had for the last two years.

Snow whipped at his face as they drove down the mountain, skirting the edge of the avalanche trail. They passed downed trees and boulders that stuck out like icebergs until, finally, they reached the road. It was covered with the same coarse chunks of snow, which a large bulldozer was slowly moving off the road, down the hill.

They continued to descend, finding the last of the avalanche's path, then turned uphill toward the resort. Michael could feel the exhaustion of the tumultuous day in his whole body as he held on to Cassie. How much longer could he stay upright? *As long as it takes to make sure Ellie is safe.*

The road was smoother and they zipped along as the lights from the resort came into sight. Finally. Cassie pulled the snowmobile up through a familiar circular driveway and, when she came to a stop, Michael climbed off and pulled off his helmet, wincing at the pain in his side.

She gave him a wary look. "You sure you don't need help?"

"No, but thanks for everything you did for me. You saved my life." People didn't survive bear attacks. He had been blessed with her presence.

She smiled. "I guess I am glad I met you."

Cassie waved and continued around the circular drive,

down the road. Michael made his way to the building. The front doors slid open, letting out a tantalizingly warm burst of air. A faint hint of music played in the background. Michael raced toward the concierge desk. A woman wearing a long braid and a welcoming smile greeted him. But her smile faded as she took him in. Michael followed her gaze downward and registered what she was looking at. His white T-shirt was sticking out from under his coat and it was stained with blood. Quickly, he tried to tuck it into his pants, but it was too painful to move his torso.

"May I call our medical team for you?" she asked.

"Not now." He waved off her comment. "My name is Michael. Did someone named Ellie leave a message for me? Striking red hair, freckles…"

The woman stared at him like she was debating whether to ignore his dismissal and call for help. She frowned and turned back to her computer. She tapped at the keys then opened the desk's top drawer and sifted through papers as Michael's heart pounded.

"I'm sorry, but I don't see anything," she said. "Do you have a room number? I can check there."

Michael shook his head. Ellie was still out. He had to try to find her. "Is Aman Gupta working here tonight?"

"He usually gets off at seven, but he might still be here because of the road closure," she said, "Let me check."

The woman picked up the phone and Michael unzipped his jacket for a look at his wound, burning at his side. He cringed as he peered at the blood-soaked material. Not good. But he'd take care of it after he knew Ellie was safe. As he zipped up his jacket, the walkie-talkie on the desk crackled to life.

"Staff, we have a code 119 in the kitchen of La Cucina. I repeat, we have code 119 in the kitchen of La Cucina."

Michael stared at the device on the desk. He had a bad, bad feeling about this.

"Where is La Cucina?" he asked.

The woman gave him skeptical look but, after a pause, she answered. "It's straight back through the lodge, on the pedestrian walkway."

"Thank you," he said. "And if you find Aman, tell him Michael Tang is looking for him. It's an emergency."

The woman's eyebrows shot up. "Sir?"

But Michael was already running for the back of the lobby. A tiny dog barked at him as he passed a couple sitting on the plush leather sofa in front of the fireplace. He raced across the carpet, down the steps and through the hallway, and then burst out the back doors of the lodge. The night was alive with the swirl of wind and snow. His side throbbed, and he was afraid to look at how much blood had leaked from his wound. He crossed a little plaza and then scanned the stores alongside the walkway in front of him, searching for the restaurant. Finally, he saw the La Cucina sign hanging from a storefront.

Michael dashed through the door and into the dining area. The room was still and quiet except for the accordion music playing in the background. No one was eating, and everyone was staring at him. Michael turned to the hostess.

"The 119. Where is it?" he asked.

The woman pointed to the double doors in back, which were flanked by two men and three women in chefs' whites. One glanced through the window on one of the doors then turned back to him. Michael ran through the dining hall toward the doors.

"Get away from me." The voice filtered through entry to the kitchen, and Michael's heart stuttered in his chest. *Ellie.* She was here. *She's alive.* And she was in trouble.

He ran through the doors and froze. Ellie and Aidan were in the rear of the space, and two staff members dressed in kitchen whites stood at a distance, behind one of the stainless steel counters, like they were unsure of the next move. They fled out the doors when Michael stepped in. Aidan had his back to Michael, and Ellie was swinging a frying pan at him. Michael ignored the searing in his side and sprinted across the room.

As Aidan turned around, Michael jumped on him. Aidan rammed him into the stainless-steel counter, sending a large bowl of lettuce skidding over the surface. It hit the floor and together they fell on top of it.

Michael's side screamed with pain. He couldn't take on this man like he had back in Ellie's house. Not in this state. He was going to let her down, but he couldn't bear that. He had made it this far—he couldn't let his body give up now. The only hope was to distract Aidan long enough for her to escape.

"Run, Ellie," he gritted out.

"Michael." Her voice sounded like a prayer, breathless and desperate. She was standing just a few feet away, frozen, but the sound of his voice seemed to spur her into action. "I'm not going anywhere without you. I'm not leaving you again."

In her voice, he heard determination, but he heard something else. Something he couldn't begin to interpret.

Aidan was flailing beneath him, the lettuce scattering across the floor as he maneuvered out from under Michael then grabbed at his arm. Michael twisted until his arm was free, but Aidan's elbow landed on his side where the bullet had hit him. Michael howled in pain.

"No!" yelled Ellie as she brought the frying pan down on Aidan's knee.

The man barked out a curse, and Ellie hit him again. She whacked him on the other knee, and the elbow, until Aidan rolled away. Michael scrambled up out of Aidan's grip, but as he turned around, Aidan had already pulled out his gun.

"Leave," he said, swinging the gun in the direction of the kitchen staff.

They fled, and Aidan turned back to Michael.

"Last time I made the mistake of leaving you to die," he hissed, low enough that Michael could barely hear him. "This time I won't make the same mistake. All those people outside the door think I'm protecting them from Elizabeth. Everyone saw you chasing me in here, so I'll call it self-defense."

Michael crouched against the shelves, the cold metal at his back. He knew Aidan wouldn't hesitate to shoot; the man had already thought through how to cover his tracks. It didn't matter whether the law was behind Aidan or not if Michael didn't live.

Michael looked up at Ellie, just a few steps away. Her face was clouded in fear.

Aidan shook his head, catching his attention. "You know I can get away with this."

FOURTEEN

Ellie's breath had been stuck in her throat from the moment she had seen the blood on the shirt peeking out from the bottom of Michael's jacket. Aidan's shot in the forest had found Michael, but somehow, Michael had found his way back to her. There was no way she was going to let him get shot again.

"Don't you dare," she said as she stepped in front of the gun, holding the frying pan in front of her like a shield.

Aidan looked up at her in surprise just as she swung the pan at his hand. The gun went off, and Ellie's heart stopped. There was a splintering crash and then shards of glass rained down. The light above her had shattered. Shrieks came through the dining room doors, but no one entered. The shock on Aidan's face turned to anger and, to Ellie's horror, she saw that he was still holding the gun. And now he was pointing it at her.

Ellie closed her eyes and drew in a breath as a calm spread through her. If this was what God wanted, she could face it. *Please let Michael survive.*

But a thud behind her startled her out of her prayer. She opened her eyes to see the kitchen doors fling open. A man in a suit ran through them, with two security guards behind him.

"These people are attacking me," said Aidan.

Ellie opened her mouth to protest, but the man in a suit spoke first.

"Sir, put down the gun."

The scrape of chairs, thud of boots against the floors and low, urgent murmurs came from the dining room. From behind her on the kitchen floor, she heard Michael blow out a breath. "Aman. Thank God."

Aman. The friend Michael had mentioned when they were back at the fire tower. Somehow, he had found them.

Aidan looked over his shoulder at the man in the suit, to the security guards, pointing their weapons at him, then back at Michael. Understanding registered in his expression. It wasn't going to work this time. "This is a misunderstanding. I want to talk to my lawyer."

One of the security guards arched her eyebrows. "That's your right. But right now, you need to hand over your gun."

Aidan glared at Ellie. She had no idea what he was going to do. Would he shoot her, right here, in front of witnesses? Her heart pounded harder.

Finally, he lowered the gun and muttered, "This isn't over."

One of the security guards came quickly to take the gun, and the other reached for his arm.

"You can't arrest me," he growled.

"You're on private property," said the woman. "We have the right to detain you until the police show up."

"We'll see how that goes," Aidan said. He smiled at Ellie as he was led away.

She could see he was already calculating how to manipulate the situation. But for right now, they were safe, so she focused on that and turned around to face Michael.

The man with the suit was kneeling down beside Michael, the man he had called Aman.

"You've been shot," he said. "I'm coordinating with our medical team. The moment Natanya, our concierge, said your name and that you were bleeding…" Aman shook his head, like he had no idea how to complete that sentence.

"It's really good to see you," Michael croaked. His smile was weak, but there were traces of humor in his voice. "You're looking great."

"You aren't," said Aman. "This is a heck of a way to say hello after three years."

"I've had quite a day."

Aman blew out a breath. "Are you going to make it here for a few minutes?"

"I'd like to think so."

"I'm going to talk to the medical team," Aman said then disappeared, leaving Ellie alone with Michael. She knelt beside him on the floor.

"How are we going to get you to the hospital?" she said. "The roads are blocked."

"I don't know," he said. After a pause, he added, "It's in God's hands."

Ellie inhaled a shaky breath.

"Thank God, you're still alive," she said. *Please, God, don't take him from his family.*

"You were ready to take a bullet for me," he said, his voice soft with a hint of amazement.

Ellie wasn't sure what to say. She looked down at the bits of lettuce stuck to his jacket, brushing them away as she processed what Michael had said. When Aidan had pointed the gun at him, she'd reacted on instinct—the instinct to protect a person she cared about.

"He threatened us with a gun, but he told everyone that I was the threat. I'm worried he'll explain it all away," she said. "The story behind it is hearsay, his word against ours. And he can twist everything to…"

Her voice faded away as Michael stroked her arm.

"That's the good thing about getting shot," said Michael, the corners of his mouth quirking up into the faintest hint of a smile. "Never thought I'd say those words."

Ellie blinked as understanding registered. "He shot you from behind."

"I think the bullet just grazed me." Michael reached for his left side, then winced and slumped back against the counter. "If I had it in me, it would have been more solid evidence."

"I'd rather pass on the evidence if it means your wound is easier to treat," she said quietly.

It hurt to look at the pain in his expression, and something shifted deep inside her. Ellie felt a surge of emotions building, emotions she wasn't prepared to think about. Emotions she'd told herself back in the police car she'd keep at bay. It was easier to focus on the threat that still lingered.

"Your friend witnessed him threatening us with a gun, too," she said. "I hope it's enough."

"You're not alone," said Michael. "We're in this together."

"I guess you're stuck with me," she said, trying to smile, trying to hold back her alarm at how quickly his energy seemed to be fading.

Michael shook his head and he rested his hand on hers. She looked at the hand covering hers, callused from hard work, then back into his dark brown eyes.

"I know it started that way, when I found you on the mountain, but this has become something else for me" he said. His eyes were filled with so much warmth and understanding, a balm against the worries that threatened to crowd in. "I want to be by your side. And I don't just mean in fighting to stop Aidan."

Ellie bit her lip as her heart pounded in her chest, as warmth flooded through her. Michael felt this connection, too, something beyond the race for their safety. How could she feel so strongly for someone she had just met—and only six months after Sean's death?

Before she could put any of these thoughts into words, the doors to the kitchen opened and a woman strode in with an Afro and a blue jumpsuit with Air Evac stitched on the breast. Behind her was a gurney stretcher, followed by another woman with a long braid down her back.

"Michael Tang?" said the first woman. "We're going to airlift you to the hospital. It's a service Miner's Peak Resort provides for its guests, and Aman tells me that you were just about to check into a room."

Ellie closed her eyes and breathed a sigh of relief. *Thank you, God.*

Michael's hand still rested on hers, and she didn't want to break the connection, but she turned her palm against his and squeezed his hand. Then she forced herself to move away. The two medics helped him onto the gurney, and she fought against the tears that threatened to well in her eyes. Ellie had so much to say to him. It was overwhelming, and she didn't know if she was ready to speak in front of all these strangers. Besides, her feelings weren't what was important right now. Michael needed to get to the hospital.

"I'll be waiting for you," she said as he lay back on the gurney.

Michael met her gaze and gave her a small nod, and then he was wheeled out the door.

"You've lost a lot of blood," said the medic with the long braid. "I'm giving you 250 milliliters, which we're hoping will stabilize you for the ride."

Michael nodded. The wooziness had set in the moment security had taken Aidan away. Michael had pushed the feeling aside as long as he could, but now that Ellie was out of danger, he could feel how close he was to drifting off. The thought sent a jolt of panic through him. What if something happened and he never woke up? There were things he hadn't said, things he needed to say.

"May I use my phone?" he said to the woman with the Afro as she took his blood pressure on his other side.

"I'm sorry, but phone calls aren't allowed for safety reasons."

Michael nodded. "Do you have a piece of paper and a pen?"

The woman nodded and rummaged through her bag.

Michael had told Ellie how he had felt, and though she hadn't answered, he felt comforted that she knew. But since Sunny's death, there had been so much distance between him and his parents. Michael couldn't bear to leave things this way.

The woman pulled out a notebook and handed it to him, along with a pen.

"Thank you," he said, and he began to write. He apologized to his parents for not being a good enough son to them, for planning to leave behind the ranch that the family had worked so hard for. A ranch that might not make it if he didn't help them. He apologized that he had made a plan that wouldn't honor them as their son, and he promised that if he made it through, he would be there for them. He would continue to work the ranch that their family had struggled so hard to get. But if he didn't make it, he asked them to watch out for Ellie. For his sake.

Michael finished the letter, folded it and handed it to the

woman. "Can you please make sure this letter stays with my belongings?"

She nodded.

It's in God's hands.

His own words had surprised him back on the kitchen floor. Now, he found that he was praying. Michael prayed, all the way to the hospital, and he prayed as he was wheeled into surgery. He prayed for his mother and father, for his grandparents, his aunts and uncles. He prayed for Isabel and the rest of the staff at Tang Ranch. And he prayed for Ellie. Always Ellie.

It had been so long since he'd talked to God, and if this was his end, he wanted this connection. *It's in Your hands.*

FIFTEEN

Ellie waited anxiously outside the door of the hospital room. She'd rushed over as soon as she could, but when the nurse had told her that Michael's family was visiting, she'd hesitated. His parents, most likely. After pulling their son into danger that led him to the emergency room, would she be welcome?

That hesitation warred with her worst fears. She had no idea what condition Michael was in. The bullet, the loss of blood, the trauma of exposure... All of it would have taken a toll on him. Maybe she should give him some privacy—

Ellie's thoughts were interrupted as the door to Michael's room swung open and a woman walked out. She was shorter than Ellie, but she looked like Michael. The same pronounced cheekbones, the same wide-set, dark brown eyes... Was this his mother?

The woman looked at Ellie and tilted her head to the side.

Ellie swallowed as her heart pounded in her chest. Too late to retreat.

"Ellie?"

"Yes. Mrs. Tang?"

The woman nodded.

"How is Michael?" The question burst out of her. "I've been so worried."

"He's recovering." His mother's voice was soft. "The doctor says it'll take some time, but he shouldn't have any lasting damage."

Ellie closed her eyes and gave a little prayer. *Thank You, Lord.* Then she opened her eyes and met Michael's mother's gaze, steeling herself for whatever came next. His mother had every reason to be angry with her for endangering her son, and all Ellie could offer was an apology. As little as it was, she had to try.

"I am so sorry for what I put your son through," she whispered. "I tried to talk him out of coming with me, but in the end, I guess that doesn't matter since he was the one who got hurt."

Mrs. Tang did the last thing Ellie expected. She smiled. "Michael has a very strong will. When he makes up his mind, no one can dissuade him of whatever it is he wants to do."

His mother didn't sound angry at all, which made her wonder if Michael's parents had heard the whole story. Ellie didn't know where to start.

"If I hadn't asked him to take me to my house, my brother-in-law never would have gone after Michael," she tried to explain. "I wish I could take that back."

Mrs. Tang shook her head. "I don't wish for that."

Ellie blinked at her in surprise. "Why not?"

"Michael has been lost to us since his wife died." Sadness weighed heavily in her voice. "I think he told you about Sunny."

Ellie nodded.

"We all mourned her, but it changed Michael. He rarely speaks anymore, and he was going to move away." Her voice broke and she paused before continuing. "His father and I arrived at the hospital when he was in surgery and were given a note, apologizing for planning to leave our ranch behind. He wrote that he changed his mind. My husband and I... We were too scared to hope. So, we waited, holding on to that letter until he was out of surgery.

"What I saw when he returned to consciousness was pieces of the Michael I knew. The man who was capable of joy as well as sorrow." His mother's eyes lit up as she spoke. "I don't know why, but this experience has brought our son back to us."

Ellie stared at the woman, speechless. It was hard to believe that a day full of fear and harm could bring something good, too. It was impossible to know the why of any of this, but it all fit together, in ways that she never could have guessed.

Mrs. Tang reached for Ellie's hands and took them in hers. The woman's fingers were soft and cool, and somehow this simple gesture sent a rush of comfort. Relief.

"The letter also mentioned you," the woman added. "He cares for you. He wanted us to protect you if he didn't make it."

"Thank you for telling me," Ellie whispered. "I care about him, too. I was sick with worry that I had taken your son away from you."

Mrs. Tang squeezed Ellie's hands. "It's the opposite. You've led him back to us."

As the hospital staff rushed around them, Ellie bowed her head in wonder at this new connection that was growing inside her. The door to Michael's room opened again and a man with salt-and-pepper hair walked out. He didn't look much like Michael but he was tall like his son. Mrs. Tang let go of Ellie's hands and turned to him.

"This is Ellie," she said, and Michael's father reached for Ellie's hand. She shook it.

"You're welcome at the ranch anytime," he said.

"Thank you. I'd be honored."

Michael's parents said their goodbyes and walked away down the hall, leaving her alone in front of Michael's door. Her heartbeat sped up at the thought of seeing him again. This felt like more than just a visit. The last time they had spoken, Michael had told her he wanted something with her, something more, and she wanted to tell him that she did, too. However Michael responded, this felt like a new chapter in her life, and she found herself hoping so much that it would be with him. She had no idea where it would lead, but she found that she was ready for it. So, with a deep breath, she placed her hand on the handle and opened the door.

Michael closed his eyes as his father walked out the door, exhausted, but happy. He was finally able to be the son he wanted to be for his parents, and he could feel the happiness it brought them. The pall that Sunny's death had cast over their relationship had lifted, and he could hear in their voices that they felt it, too. His father talked about ideas for the ranch, and the ways they could rely on tourist dollars for the summer, during Michael's recovery. He wanted to plan together, and they had plenty of time for that.

When the handle of the door turned again, Michael scanned the room to see if his parents had forgotten something. But it wasn't his parents who walked through the door. It was Ellie. Michael's heart jumped in his chest.

She looked different, dressed like the woman he had seen fleeing down the mountain in an expensive-looking white blouse and gray trousers. But unlike on the mountain, she looked put together. Her long red hair was pulled into a neat bun at the base of her neck, and she wore pearl earrings, a pearl necklace and pale lipstick.

This is the real her. She wasn't the woman he had spent

that day with, the woman he had felt close to. She lived a different life than he did. It was a life he had left behind when he and Sunny had decided to move to the ranch, a life he'd decided he wasn't interested in anymore. He had to remember that throughout this conversation, no matter how good it felt to see her again.

"Michael," she whispered. "May I come in?"

She looked nervous, almost shy.

"I'd love that," he said. "You can pull up a chair."

Another thought occurred to him as he watched her cross the floor. The last time he'd spoken to her, he had told her how he'd felt. Was she here out of guilt, out of obligation, or was there something more? Michael wanted it to be something more so badly.

Ellie pulled a beige chair up to the side of his bed. "You're sitting up."

"Just barely," he said. "I'm supposed to avoid moving this side for the next couple days."

She bit her lip, so quiet. And suddenly he wasn't sure what to say to her without pushing her, prying.

"I'm pressing charges," said Michael. "He shot me once, and hotel security found him aiming the gun at me. I hope that's enough to outweigh whatever friendships he has in town."

"The police granted me a restraining order, and when we went back to the house, I got an escort. I've been working to dig up all the emails between Sean and Aidan. There was a trail of messages that allude to the bribes and payments, and I'm hoping that's enough to take to some sort of authority. I think Clint is involved, too, but I'm not sure if I have evidence of it."

"The police came in to take a statement about Aidan," he

said. "But they said they hadn't charged him yet, just took him in for questioning. I've been so worried about you."

She nodded. "I've been staying in the resort. When your friend heard about the situation, he offered me that room you were supposedly staying in. He said since it's late season, they're not fully booked, so it's not a problem if I want to stay there for a little while. Aidan is barred from the resort, and they've sent his photo around to all the staff."

He understood that the police had their own way of working, and he believed that people should be treated innocent until proven guilty, but in this case, it left Ellie vulnerable. Thank God, his community was stepping in to help protect her. He wished he could be the one watching out for her, but this was the next best option for now.

"Thank God for Aman," said Michael, closing his eyes.

"I thought you weren't so sure about your relationship with God," she said, a hint of a grin on her face.

"These last few days have made me reconsider," he said, trying to smile.

He was coming to realize that it was a journey. His relationship with God was just that—a relationship, ongoing, with highs and lows. Michael may never fully understand Sunny's death, and the ache of it would never go away. All relationships included trials, and his relationship with God seemed to have survived. Maybe it could be stronger after these trials. That's where Michael hoped he was headed.

"I'm never going to get over Sean's death," said Ellie.

Michael nodded as his heart sank. Of course, he knew she wouldn't, but was this her way of signaling there was no possibility of a new relationship with him? Michael had wondered if this was where everything would lead, but he had hoped it wouldn't come so fast. He just wanted to sit with her for a while. Still, he forced himself to say, "I know. I will never get over Sunny either."

Because that was the truth, too. So why did it feel different for him right now?

"I've been thinking a lot about that over the last few days, since I watched you get carried away from me on that gurney, not knowing where you were going, or what happened to you," she said.

"I understand," he forced himself to say. "We barely know each other."

She gave a little laugh. "I don't even have your phone number."

Michael nodded, trying to keep his disappointment off his face.

Ellie took a deep breath then let it out. "All of these things should be the reasons why you and I can't be anything more than friends. That should be the reason why I say goodbye to you right now, or say that maybe we could just be friends. But that's not how I feel. I feel all of those things can be true…including that I have room in my heart to care about you someday. As something more than a friend."

Michael's heart soared. Was he hearing correctly? Maybe this was some sort of postsurgery dream. Did she feel this way, too, that love between them might be possible? Maybe this was part of what his minister had meant so long ago when he had said that love was infinite. Michael had loved Sunny with all his heart, and this feeling wasn't about the past or his mistakes, or what he did wrong. This was simply more love.

His gaze was fixed on Ellie, and her cheeks grew pink. "Or maybe I am too late? Maybe you've reconsidered what you said back on the kitchen floor?"

"Not at all," said Michael quickly with a laugh. "You

do have me wondering if I'm having some sort of postsurgery hallucination."

Ellie laughed and then she stood up. She came closer and sat on the edge of his bed. She lay her hand on his, the way he had touched her back at the resort. "This is real," she whispered.

This *was* real. And it was what he wanted. He felt it was right in the deepest parts of him. He knew it.

"Even before all this happened, I'd been thinking about moving, getting rid of both houses," she said. "The house in Santa Barbara has so many memories of Sean. He had wanted to move there for the business. As an accountant, I could get work wherever I wanted, so I just followed him. And now this Tahoe house…"

"You always have a place to stay at the ranch."

"Your father said the same thing."

Michael's eyebrows shot up in surprise. "He did? He's usually a little more on the reserved side. At least until you get to know him."

"Now I know where you get that from," she said.

Michael smiled.

"Our first date was pretty intense," he said, and she laughed. "How about we do something a little quieter next time? Like dinner and a movie?"

"Or dinner and a horseback ride?" she suggested. "Of the many things I took away from that crazy day, I realized how much I miss horseback riding."

"Among many things," he said wryly.

Her hand was warm on top of his. It was a connection that he didn't want to break.

"Would you go on a date with me, Ellie? It might just be dinner." He gestured at his side. "But I hope we'll be able to ride together soon, too."

"I would love that." A flush rose to her cheeks as she held his gaze.

Then she leaned forward and brushed her lips against his. The kiss was warm, tender and filled with promise, and his heart pounded in his chest. This kiss felt like the beginning of something, something that could last. A week ago, Michael would never have believed it was possible. Now, everything seemed possible.

EPILOGUE

One year later

"Is that all you're bringing?" Michael asked from the doorway of their new bedroom.

Ellie glanced up, basking in the warmth of her husband's dark eyes, then looked down at the backpack dangling from her hand. "You said there was hiking, so I should just bring a backpack…"

"You could have gone with a camping pack," he said, pointing at the one he carried on his back. "Or maybe I overpacked? It's going to be cold."

Ellie laughed. "You can say you brought the warmest socks, if you're looking for an excuse."

"Or I'll tell our parents that I'm carrying your extra clothes, just to be a gentleman," he said, smiling.

She gave him a little shove, but he caught her hand in his. He laced his fingers with hers and she smiled up at him, his deep brown eyes full of both love and mischief.

"Also, most of my clothes are all packed," she added, gesturing to the moving boxes that lined the wall.

Ellie gazed around at their beautiful new home, where they'd just spent the first night of their new life together. It was hard to believe they were finally married.

Shortly after they'd gotten engaged, they'd taken the money from the sale of Ellie's Santa Barbara home and built a house, just for them, on the Tang Ranch property. They'd chosen a spot farther down the river, in the forest, a short hike from the rest of the buildings. It was a two-story, A-frame house, with wooden siding and a wide front porch. It was big enough for the two of them and maybe more. Someday.

"Ready for a last goodbye to our parents?" she asked.

"They seem to be doing just fine without us around," said Michael, taking her backpack with his free hand.

"True," she said with a bit of wonder in her voice.

But maybe it shouldn't have been a surprise. Ellie's parents, ranchers who had only visited Ellie in Santa Barbara twice, had surprised her by accepting Michael's parents' invitation to stay at the ranch for a week, both before and after the wedding, in Michael and Sunny's former home. They had never once accepted Sean's parents' invitations to visit, though Ellie suspected that the ranch felt less intimidating than Clint and Janine's rambling Silicon Valley mansion. Either way, the two families had hit it off, making both Michael and Ellie a lot less nervous about leaving for their honeymoon. For the past year, she'd had more connection with her parents than she had during her entire marriage with Sean. Maybe it was that she had been on her own, or maybe it was that their worlds were not so different now. Whatever the reason, she was grateful.

As they walked out of their new home and down the snowy driveway toward the main ranch house, she thought of how much had changed. Not only had she sold the Santa Barbara house shortly after her hospital visit with Michael, but she had also moved out of the house in Tahoe, ready for a fresh start. She had kept the cabin in the Virgin Is-

lands that Sean had set up as a safe house. Maybe someday she and Michael would visit, but she wasn't quite ready
for that yet.

Aidan, thankfully, had been arrested, tried and found
guilty of attempted murder. It had taken time—and a restraining order—and Aidan had done his best to try the
case in the court of local public opinion. But in the end,
she'd been vindicated. The emails and "gifts" to the council members, along with her testimony, Michael's, Aman's
and the rest of the hotel staff's had stood together against
the story that Aidan had concocted, the one where he'd insisted that somehow he'd been the victim.

Clint Alexander was never charged for anything, though
Ellie was almost sure he wasn't completely innocent. After
Aidan's conviction, he had first tried to reconcile with her.
When that didn't work, he had asked to buy her out of the
company. She had offered him a counterdeal: she'd take
nothing from the company, but an independent firm of her
choice would look over all future environmental reports before any project began. She had left that chapter of her life
behind, but with the confidence that Green Living Construction would no longer cause harm.

That wasn't the only change. She had moved to Clover Valley and started a consultant practice from her tiny
apartment on the main street of the little mountain town
and, for the first time in her life, she'd lived completely on
her own. Slowly, the world had blossomed in front of her.
On the weekends, she'd spent time at Tang Ranch, helping
with the horses or riding with Michael, learning the land.
Over the last year, she had watched Michael open slowly,
his smiles becoming more frequent, and she'd found herself
smiling more often, too. Now, when she looked over at her
new husband, so playful and affectionate, she barely rec-

ognized him from the silent, withdrawn man she had met a year ago. Ellie had to wonder if he was thinking something similar about her.

They walked up the steps to the main house and when they opened the door, the front hallway was filled with the sounds of their parents' voices. Michael set their bags on the floor and they entered the living room. Four plush armchairs circled a cracking fire in the stone fireplace. Ellie's mother was leaning over the armrest in deep conversation with Mrs. Tang, and her father was laughing at something Mr. Tang had said.

When Mrs. Tang caught sight of the pair, she stopped talking and gestured to them. "The newlyweds!"

All four parents rose from their seats and headed for Michael and her. Ellie's father got to her first and wrapped her in a warm embrace.

"Are you sure this is what you want to do for your honeymoon?" he asked. "You could go somewhere warm."

Ellie suppressed a smile. "We're sure."

"I love you, sweetheart," he whispered as he released her.

Then he turned to Michael and shook her husband's hand. "You make my daughter happy, and I am forever thankful you came into our lives."

Ellie's mother and Michael's parents crowded in. Michael's mother fussed with Ellie's scarf, making sure it covered her neck.

"Have a wonderful honeymoon," said Mrs. Tang. "And welcome to the family."

"Thank you, Mrs. Tang."

Her mother-in-law's eyes sparkled. "Please, call me Mother."

Ellie swallowed back a lump in her throat. Never could

she have imagined she'd experience this warmth and joy of togetherness.

"Thank you, Mother," she whispered.

When Ellie had first suggested the fire lookout tower as their honeymoon destination, Michael had thought she was joking. But the more he'd considered it, the more he'd liked the idea. It was a part of their story together, the first day they'd met, and in the many times they'd gone over that day that changed both their lives, she had confessed that when they'd sat at the table, she had felt something more than just gratefulness. Even if neither of them had realized it on that day, it had been the start of something new. He, too, had seen her as more than a woman in distress. Looking back, he had to agree that maybe he could even say that it was the beginning of his falling in love with her. So they'd planned a tiny wedding, followed by a honeymoon at the tower.

Now, as he snowshoed up the trail with his cross-country skis and two gallons of water hanging from his pack, he reconsidered the wisdom of this idea. Weren't honeymoons supposed to be for relaxing? Then again, he had the most beautiful view in the world: the snow-covered mountain, the clear sky at dusk, and his new wife, trekking ahead of him.

"There it is," said Ellie over her shoulder.

Michael took a couple more steps and then he could see it, too. The fire tower peeked out from behind the tall pines.

Ellie picked up the pace as they approached. It was just how it had been a year ago, though today there was a little less snow. They climbed the snowy steps, and Michael punched in the code and then opened the door into their little paradise. At least, it would be paradise once he got the propane stove running.

Ellie kicked off her boots and crossed the room to the table in the corner for two. She set her backpack on the ground and pulled out the thermos of hot chocolate, setting it on the blue-and-white-checked tablecloth. Michael unlaced his boots and walked over to join her.

They stood facing the windows. Ellie unscrewed the lid of the thermos, and poured hot liquid into the tiny metal cup then handed it to him. He took a sip, savoring the sweet taste, warming his insides. He should really start the stove, but Michael wanted to savor this moment in the quiet cabin, just the two of them. The sun was setting far off in the distance, somewhere over the mountains and down in the valley, and the sky was lit with a rainbow of colors, red, orange, yellow shifting into deep blues and purples above them.

"Was it worth the hike?" Ellie asked. "I think I might've heard a few mumbles on the way up."

Michael chuckled. "Who, me? Never."

Ellie laughed that bright, musical laugh. He had heard it so many times over the last year, and it filled him with a warmth that glowed inside him when they were together.

"How are you doing, Mrs. Tang?"

Ellie blushed, and she couldn't hold back her smile. "I'm still getting used to my new last name."

He was still getting used to being married again. It was so strange, and yet so natural.

"I love you, Ellie," he whispered. "I'm so grateful we found each other."

He reached for her hand, and the new ring on her fourth finger pressed against his skin as she squeezed his hand. She turned and stood on her tiptoes, tilting her head up to-

ward Michael's face. He looked down into her dark gray
eyes then brushed his lips against hers.

"I love you, Elizabeth May Tang," he whispered.

More than he ever thought would be possible after a
devastating loss. He couldn't pretend he understood the
direction his life had taken, but it brought him to this moment, his hope renewed, his love for Ellie so strong. Once
again, he had faith in the future. But most of all, he wanted
to hold on to this moment right now. He wanted to savor
every minute of this joyful day.

* * * * *

If you enjoyed Danger on the Peaks
by Rebecca Hopewell
Check out High-Stakes Blizzard
Available now from Love Inspired!

And discover more on
LoveInspired.com

Dear Reader,

I have always loved amnesia stories. As I read, I'm on the edge of my chair, looking for clues about the characters' pasts. Writing an amnesia story got me to explore more deeply what this experience would be like. The idea I kept coming back to was this: I would be terrified if it happened to me! Our experiences and memories are how we make sense of the world, so without them, every moment is a step into the unknown.

Ellie must negotiate this fear of the unknown as she figures out who is chasing her and why. Luckily, she finds someone she can trust in Michael. He is struggling with the opposite problem: how to live with the crushing weight of his memories. Neither Ellie nor Michael is looking to fall in love, but maybe love is exactly what they both need...

Happy reading!
Rebecca